FARIDA

ESSENTIAL TRANSLATIONS SERIES 34

Guernica Editions Inc. acknowledges the support of
the Canada Council for the Arts and the Ontario Arts Council.
The Ontario Arts Council is an agency of the Government of Ontario.
We acknowledge the financial support of the Government of Canada through the
National Translation Program for Book Publishing for our translation activities.
We also acknowledge the financial support of the Government of Canada
through the Canada Book Fund (CBF) for our publishing activities.

ONTARIO ARTS COUNCIL
CONSEIL DES ARTS DE L'ONTARIO

an Ontario government agency
un organisme du gouvernement de l'Ontario

Naïm Kattan

FARIDA

Translated by Norman Cornett
& Antonio D'Alfonso

GUERNICA

TORONTO – BUFFALO – LANCASTER (U.K.)
2015

First published in French in 1991 as *Farida*
Copyright © 1991 Les Éditions Hurtubise
Translation copyright © 2015, Norman Cornett,
Antonio D'Alfonso and Guernica Editions Inc.
All rights reserved. The use of any part of this publication,
reproduced, transmitted in any form or by any means, electronic,
mechanical, photocopying, recording or otherwise stored in a
retrieval system, without the prior consent of the publisher is an
infringement of the copyright law.

Michael Mirolla, editor
Guernica Editions Inc.
1569 Heritage Way Oakville, (ON), Canada L6M 2Z7
2250 Military Road, Tonawanda, N.Y. 14150-6000 U.S.A.

Distributors:
University of Toronto Press Distribution,
5201 Dufferin Street, Toronto (ON), Canada M3H 5T8
Gazelle Book Services, White Cross Mills, High Town, Lancaster LA1 4XS U.K.

First edition.
Printed in Canada.

Legal Deposit – First Quarter
Library of Congress Catalog Card Number: 2015930123
Library and Archives Canada Cataloguing in Publication
Kattan, Naïm, 1928-
[Farida. English]
Farida / Naïm Kattan; translated from the French by
Norman Cornett & Antonio D'Alfonso.
(Essential translations series ; 34)
Translation of: Farida.
Novel.
Issued in print and electronic formats.
ISBN 978-1-77183-038-6 (pbk.).
ISBN 978-1-77183-039-3 (epub).
ISBN 978-1-77183-040-9 (mobi)
I. Cornett, Norman; D'Alfonso, Antonio, translators II. Title. III. Title: Farida.
English IV. Series: Essential translations series ; 34
PS8571.A872F3713 2015   C843'.54
C2015-900294-X   C2015-900295-8

THE NEWS HIT THE JEWISH community like a bombshell. The newspapers' headlines gave rise to a combination of panic, shame, and consternation:

Sasson Karkoukli – Murdered by Ismaïl Hassan – Arrested with Bloody Knife in Hand – The Murderer Accuses Salim Abdullah of hiring him to Commit the Crime.

Jews hid to read the newspapers, savouring the sordid details that made goose bumps rise on their flesh. The murder had taken place inside a slaughterhouse. Sasson was making his usual rounds, greeting *chohets* (the ritual butchers), and talking it up with the workers. While alone and busy selecting some of the choice animals for himself, he was jumped by Ismaïl. Holding Sasson in a head-lock with one arm, he slit his throat with the other. Sasson fell limp next to the freshly slaughtered sheep, his blood mingling with that of the animals.

Twenty-year-old Ismaïl Hassan had been in Sasson's employ for six months. Each morning this frail young man brought coffee to Sasson's office in the slaughterhouse. Sasson paid him well: three dinars a month, as well as tips and gifts. And Ismaïl never went home empty-handed. He always had a choice cut of meat stashed somewhere on his person.

The newspaper did not identify the witness who claimed that Ismaïl gathered up the pieces of meat that the chohets rejected (on account of broken bones, etc.) and sold them under the table. The police launched a man-hunt for the victim's brother-in-law and business partner, Salim Abdullah, accused of having hired the hit-man.

Although not as favourable to Jews as *Al Zaman* and its Christian owner, Tawfike Al Samaani, the newspaper *Al Bildad* nevertheless put on a friendly face towards them. It described Ismaïl's arrest thus: dagger in hand, he ran into the street thinking that no one had seen him commit this crime. However, a rabbi by the name of Shummel or Helket unexpectedly witnessed the scene and started yelling: "Murderer! Stop the murderer." The screams terrified Ismaïl and he froze in his tracks. However, Jews knew that *Al Bildad*'s supposed rabbi was but a chohet who went neither by the name of Shummel nor Helket, epithets that Muslims concocted for Jews.

At the same time dark clouds hung over the Jewish community. Yassin Al Hashimi, no friend of the Jews, had just regained power. Although he went along with the British, he tacitly approved the Nazi diktats coming out of Germany since their taking over the government three years earlier. Meanwhile, the Iraqi army's junior officers openly displayed their zeal for the Fuehrer, and *Al Bildad* published articles on the new Germany, replete with anti-Semitic statements from the Nazis.

From the day Al Hashimi took power, rumours started to run wild in the Jewish community. Shadowy kidnappers snatched a Jew from the working-class district of Abou Sifaine. Without ever naming the intended victims, people vividly recounted the attempted kidnapping of a banker, as well as that of a grocer in Al Chorja who barely escaped his assailants. Stories of Jewish children being beat up on the street also began to circulate.

But there was nothing new in this: this type of gossip had always enjoyed currency in the Jewish community. Everyone had a story to tell. Around three o'clock, while most took their mid-afternoon nap, two suspicious-looking individuals trailed a man walking alone in the Al Akoulia neighbourhood. After turning the street corner, he managed to shake them off by ducking into the entry way of a house. People no longer dared step foot in the Muslim quarters of Babel Cheikh. In any case what business did a Jew have walking on Shiite streets? Nor could the Jewish community count any longer on the British for protection. Their ambassador had found ways to distance himself from Jews. Perhaps he did this to curry favour with Iraqi nationalists. In any case, the English had long practised a policy of playing both ends against the middle.

Just days before Sasson Karkoukli's murder, the Hakham Bashi or Chief Rabbi had apparently visited the new prime minister in order to pay his respects on behalf of the Jewish community and to pledge the community's loyalty to the new government. During this meeting the Hakham Bashi asked the prime minister to offer public assurances to the shaken Jewish community whose insecurity grew with each new rumour.

Two days after the murder, *Al Zaman* splashed the prime minister's response on its front page. The government safeguards all its citizens, no matter which community they belong to and will punish any threat to the public. Although the prime minister did not mention Jews by name, everyone could read between the lines. The Jewish community breathed a sigh of relief and those who only a month before had protested in front of the Hakham Bashi's office now showered him with praise.

Their spiritual leader had assured the new prime minister that his predecessor, Hikat Soleyman, had never enjoyed the Jewish community's blessings. Well-known for his leftist leanings, Soleyman's cabinet included young ministers such as Kamel Al Chaudurchi and Abdel Kader, who both espoused socialism. Some Jews openly stated that the British ousted Soleyman because of his pronounced Marxist sympathies. In his stead they put Al Hachimi, reputed to favour Nazism.

By adding a surcharge on the sale of kosher meat, the Jewish community financed its institutions, such as the Hakham Bashi's department. It annually awarded to the highest bidder all rights to the ritual slaughter of animals and sale of their meat. Six months before Sasson's murder, the Hakham had given these rights to a friend who then for his own gain proceeded to inflate the price of meat.

Although Jews accepted being charged somewhat more for their meat, they balked at paying twice as much for it as Muslims, especially since rumour had it that some Jewish leaders received kickbacks from this arrangement. Over a hundred people showed up to demonstrate in front of the Hakham's office. The next day *Al Bildad* splashed across its front page:

Jew Protest ...

The Jewish community detested nothing more than making newspaper headlines. Gossipmongers said that the Karkoukli family was behind the staging of the demonstration. Be that as it may, six months later they won the contract for the slaughter and sale of kosher meat.

The Jewish community normally hired a Muslim company for the ritual slaughter of animals. *Chohets*, of course, butchered them according to Jewish law and the rabbinate oversaw operations. However, the company's Muslim owners set the price of meat in order to make a profit. But these outsiders to the Jewish community didn't know how to deal with the *chohets* whom they called "rabbis." As a result the Muslim company invariably partnered with Jews who, in effect, held the exclusive rights to slaughter and sell kosher meat. By marketing its name and know-how, the Muslim company consequently made money without even having to lift a finger.

Hassan al Cheikhy, a judge, and Hamid, a former minister and prominent lawyer, had an older brother named Jamil who, before moving to Baghdad, had owned a store in Kut. This brother bought businesses that the other brothers themselves couldn't or didn't want to run. Sasson knew Hamid well because he had retained him as his lawyer for a case. As well, while serving as a government minister, Hamid had proven most helpful in obtaining permits for Sasson to build, import, etc. Naturally, Hamid and those he bribed pocketed a great deal of money from these doings.

When he had first arrived in Baghdad, Jamil had epitomized the country bumpkin. He didn't drink alcohol and had never set foot in a brothel. All the city's nightclubs ran bordellos so that prostitutes were able to service customers not just in covert whorehouses. Sasson, and especially Abdullah, skilfully accustomed Jamil to the ways of the world. From then on they found it harder and harder to tear him away from these pursuits. Jamil had developed an obsession for the cabaret singers, Salimah Pacha and Nurjus Shawki. He spent night after night listening so intently to them sing that he didn't even remember to take a sip of his drink.

Jamil went to the slaughterhouse office every morning. There, he sipped tea, glanced at the paperwork pile on his desk, and waited for Sasson or Salim to come and tell him which letters, invoices, or cheques to sign. He then spent two or three hours at a café near the mosque in Haydur Khanah where, if he could find a partner, he played backgammon. After noontime prayers he returned home for lunch and a nap. All his children had married and he didn't discuss politics with his wife, a chary, fat woman who slept most of the day and, when awake, ordered the servants about.

Although unrelated, the managers of the slaughterhouse, Sasson and Salim, had proven inseparable for 15 years. So much so, their families considered them two peas in a pod.

They had met at the Eastern Bank where they had gone to work immediately after graduating from Chammac High School. Neither of them possessed the aptitude or financial wherewithal to pursue university studies.

Sasson came from a family of modest means. His father owned a fabrics shop in the bazaar which his older brother, Abraham, had inherited. His father raised the children as best he knew how and died at age 60. Two years later Abraham took over the boutique. Meantime, Sasson barely made it through high school and then took the first job he could get – cashier at the Eastern Bank. From his wicket he watched day in, day out, while client after client deposited or withdrew hundreds, if not thousands of dinars. Before long Sasson learned to sort and count bank notes in the blink of an eye, with absolute accuracy to boot!

One week before Sasson started at the bank it had hired Salim Abdullah. Salim could be found in the wicket next to Sasson. Although unfailingly polite and patient with customers, Salim remained aloof, stony-faced, seldom smiling. No wonder he initially seemed dour to Sasson. They hardly talked until the day a client claimed that Sasson had miscounted his money. Salim took the wad of bills from the customer and counted them one by one. In the end, it turned out Sasson's count had been correct. The client apologized profusely and, for the first time, Sasson heard Salim laugh. When the bank closed, Sasson invited him to a bistro.

"You don't owe me anything," Salim said.

"Pay for the drinks if you want."

They both broke out laughing. That's when their friendship began.

Salim was the second in a family with three children. Salim's older brother, Naji, still hadn't completed his studies. The faculty of medicine, which only admitted two Jews per year, didn't accept him due to his grades, and Naji's parents couldn't pay the bribes demanded for his entrance. Even the law faculty turned him down. He then failed engineering and ended up in the lowly state teachers college. Meanwhile, Naji's mother, Khatoun, had sold her jewels to cover the tuition fees for her favourite son. She gave him the best cuts of meat at meals and made sure he slept like a baby during siesta time.

As for his father, Selman, he devoted himself to the pursuit of piety. Scorning Western pants and jackets, he instead wore the zeboun, a traditional cassock that buttons in the front. Over this he, like the Bedouins, put on an *aba* (long cape) when outside. Selman received a pittance for working as Chammach at the Hakam Heskel synagogue. Khatoun's family despised Selman but helped her out financially. If she hadn't feared God's wrath, she too would have scorned him. Yet how could she fault a Jew for his piety? How could she tell him that he prayed too much when in fact he simply followed the prayer book? If he had become a rabbi she could have lived with that, even if their family wouldn't have much more money. But to remain Chammach proved a constant source of humiliation. Worse still, Selman lacked any ambition. He spent all his time thanking God for food, drink, sleep, and life. At home only Najiah, his young daughter, sided with Selman.

Khatoun so expected a third boy that when she had a girl she named her after Naji, her favourite son. She thus signified her acceptance of God's will. Najiah would have served as her namesake's punching bag if her other brother Salim hadn't decided in adolescence to take her under his wing like his father did. Although cute, she didn't possess that striking beauty which enables a young woman to marry without a dowry. She had at best an average intelligence and flunked several subjects. However, that didn't bother her parents. They had but one concern – to marry her off with as little a dowry as possible. Or better still, with none at all.

The day she turned 13, Najiah's mother began to harass her about getting married. "You'll never find a husband if you don't get up until eight o'clock in the morning. Maybe you'd land a husband if you at least knew how to iron clothes and wash dishes." Even though he too had a hard time not flunking his courses, nonetheless Salim boldly assured his sister: "I'll take care of your marriage, Najiah. Don't worry. Your brother's got your back." To this their mother cynically responded: "He'll pay for the wedding with your father's millions."

Their dad never got involved in these conversations. He only spoke about day-to-day affairs. Had they poured water into a basin for the ritual washing of hands? Had they laid the table for Shabbat? Najiah looked after her father's every need because she didn't have any other way to express her love for him. When Salim wasn't in the house, Najiah's mother and brother ganged up on her. But she didn't say a word. Dead silence proved her only defence against their verbal assaults.

As soon as Salim returned home, her spirits lifted because he always took her side.

Salim admired, if not venerated, his father, yet he also pitied his retreat into a silent world of inner happiness. To draw him out of his self-imposed solitary confinement, Salim would sometimes ask his father to explain the designated scripture reading of the week. His dad then came alive and morphed into a master communicator. His face lit up as he quoted by heart passages from Guemara, Rachi, Maimonides, and expounded on their finer points. At the end of such an exchange, he would put his hand on Salim's head and bless him.

The Abdullah family ate their meals in a small room adjacent to the kitchen. They couldn't all sit down at once without elbowing each other. In any case the mother never ate with the men. She only served them. Salim wished they lived like American families in Hollywood films where the mother and daughters sat next to the father and sons so that everyone talked and laughed together.

Salim didn't resent his mother. Since she'd lost all hope in her husband, she desperately held onto the belief that her oldest son, Naji, would work a miracle. She had a rich brother who always praised his brother-in-law when he gave his sister a small monthly allowance: "He's a pious man who fears God. He doesn't drink, gamble, smoke, or run around." That is to say he had eyes only for her. She sheepishly nodded her head in agreement and thanked her brother for his generosity. How could she tell him that her husband didn't ever look at his wife? Wouldn't she then seem shameless to her brother?

Salim only talked to his brother if he had to. Although polite, he addressed him like a stranger, or at most someone he barely knew. Salim couldn't stand that his brother had no greater ambition than to spend his life teaching in a public elementary school! And to think his mother considered him her pride and joy! She let the whole world know her plans of marrying him into a rich family whose daughter's dowry would enable Naji to live like a king. This didn't bother Salim at all. He could care less what happened to his brother. Naji didn't form part of Salim's world.

Salim had no friends at school. All his buddies dreamed of becoming doctors or engineers, but they lacked will power and came from poor families. As for himself, Salim thought only of getting rich, yet didn't have a clue how he'd make his fortune.

Convinced that someday they'd hit it rich, Sasson and Salim grabbed every spare moment between customers to brainstorm about their future. They knew that if they spent their lives at the bank they'd never have anything more than security and a meagre income. Indeed to achieve that their manager, Eliahou, had worked his tail off for 20 years. What a gyp! The poor man amounted to a hired hand whose dreams could go no further than his paltry pension.

Sasson lived in the Akd el Nassarah neighbourhood and after work he usually went home to eat. There he sat out on the roof during sunny days in the winter but napped downstairs in the summer.

Salim's family had moved from the old city to become one of the first to live in the new neighbourhood called Senak.

To avoid eating dinner with his father and brother, Salim normally stayed downtown for a while after work to have a coffee on Bank Street, or now and then, at some swanky spot on Rachid Street.

One evening at the beginning of summer, while Salim walked along the river on Abou Nouas Street, he ran into Sasson who happened to be there by himself. They spent the night debating their future. Should they pull up stakes?

WHERE WOULD THEY GO? How could they pay for the trip? Europe stood on the doorstep of war and neither Calcutta, nor Shanghai, nor Rangoon looked any better. Despite the recent howls of some extremists, Salim and Sasson concluded that their future still lay in Baghdad. To tell the truth, as long as the British held sway over Iraq, its Jews remained safe. More to the point, the Brits fully intended to keep control of Iraq's oil supplies. To succeed therefore Salim and Sasson must take up the gauntlet like others who had made it big.

After that first encounter, Salim and Sasson often ran into each other on Abou Nouas Street. These chance meetings at dusk sometimes led to playing backgammon in a café for the rest of the evening.

One day, just before the bank closed, Sasson said: "Don't leave yet. Wait for me. I need to talk to you, but not here. Let's go somewhere else, a place where nobody knows us."

The element of intrigue in Sasson's voice amused Salim. They crossed Rachid Street at the intersection with Bank Street. At the entrance to the Chora bazaar, there was a café that regularly drew a mixed bag of Kurds, tradesmen, and porters. Every day Salim walked past this coffee house and heard Kurdish, but he would never have considered going inside.

The owner didn't seem the least surprised when two gentlemen wearing business suits walked in, and they also appeared to go unnoticed by the cherwal-clad workers who frequented this café. Sasson cleverly surmised that they need not go far to have privacy. In this very public place no one paid attention to them.

The café owner served them tea. All the while Sasson said nothing.

"What gives?" Salim said.

"Do you have to hurry off?" Sasson asked.

"No, but I can't wait for you to let me in on the secret."

Sasson's cheeky smile turned into teasing laughter.

"There's no secret."

"So why make a production of it?"

"Hold your horses. We've got time."

Salim had an inkling that all this tra-la-la amounted to more than a joke or some harebrained scheme.

"Have you ever visited a whorehouse?" Sasson asked.

Flabbergasted, Salim said in disbelief: "Why ask me such a question?"

"Do you consider it off limits? I just wanted to invite you along on payday."

"That's your big secret? You could have talked to me about it at the bank."

"You seem in a rush, but I also need to talk business with you. First tell me though, will you come on payday? It's a safe place. The women have no diseases, and men say it's the best brothel in Baghdad."

"We've got time to think about this. It's only the middle of the month." Then, with a roguish grin: "Perhaps. I'm not counting it out."

Sasson slowly sipped his tea.

"And the business matter? I'll have to leave soon. I didn't tell anyone I'd be coming home late."

Sasson drew closer and started to whisper: "We've both made up our minds not to spend our lives at the bank."

"Right."

"We know each other well enough to go into business together."

He waited.

"Isn't that true?"

"Yes," Salim said.

"Well there you go. I believe we can hold down our jobs while opening up an import-export business. We'll give it a name and rent an office. Ready-made customers come to our wickets every day, and we know them."

"But what about the bank?"

"We don't need its permission. We'll begin by working at our rented office a few hours during afternoons and evenings. When the business gets off the ground we'll resign one at a time from the bank. It's a treasure trove of information. I've already found a room at an inn for two dinars a month. We might even get it for a dinar and a half. We'll need a table, chairs, and a typewriter. We won't have money to visit the whorehouse often, but who knows, maybe one of us could leave the bank in six months."

"OK," Salim said.

"Don't you want time to think about it?"

"Sasson, I'm telling you to count me in."

"Thanks, brother."

"Can we rent it today?"

"They're waiting for us to sign the lease."

They disappeared into the bowels of a bazaar. It featured rows of booths, some big enough for ten people, while others could barely fit a single person. Each boutique specialized in a certain fabric: poplin, satin, velour, etc. Everyone knew the shopkeepers by name and reputation. Except for a few Assyrians and Shiite, Jews ran this bazaar's cloth trade. Inns stood at the street corners while the central courtyard served as a warehouse surrounded by offices on the ground and first floors. These offices looked like homes. One end of this bazaar opened onto the metalworkers' market. By passing between bales of fabric and up a dark staircase, Sasson brought Salim to a storage room.

Sasson pushed the door and turned on an electric bulb that dangled from the ceiling. Its light revealed old, blackened, mouldy walls.

"The sun never shines in here so we don't need to worry about getting hot," Sasson said with a laugh.

Salim spied a wooden table and two chairs like those in the café.

"Have a seat," Sasson said, already acting as master of the house.

"I'm not tired," Salim said, feeling half embarrassed and half disappointed.

Events had unfolded at a dizzying pace. Within two hours Salim had rented an office and become the business partner of a fellow worker whose family he didn't even know. Could he trust him?

Had he dreamt that he had co-signed a lease? Perhaps by the end of the month he'd have the money to buy a new suit, but for now it remained out of the question.

Throughout that evening the new business partners walked excitedly up and down Abou Nouas Street. Indeed they showed no signs of fatigue and couldn't sit still in a café.

"I've thought of a name for our business," Sasson said.

"We can't use our own."

FARIDA

"That's right. Nor can we call it Company Limited unless we prove we have sufficient capital and officially register it. I thought of Iraq Trading Bureau because the title has a ring to it."

"Why just Iraq? That's too restrictive. How about the Middle East Trading Bureau?"

"Great idea!" Sasson exclaimed while patting Salim on the back.

For several weeks thereafter the new business partners lived in a state of frenzy. In the mornings at the bank they secretly recorded the names and addresses of its corporate customers; then during the afternoons at their office they typed the same letter to each company on the list. They offered them their services as brokers or sales representatives. They requested price lists, shipment schedules and product samples. They did mailings to England, France, Germany and the United States.

A month later replies began coming in. A few amounted to flat refusals because the company already had a broker. However, some responses proved encouraging and included catalogues, price lists and a request for a letter of reference from their bank.

After a few months they had enough offers to start looking for customers. Since they served as middlemen, they would receive a commission only if they found importers.

Believe it or not they got a letter of inquiry from their own bank. One of its corporate clients asked the bank to provide information about them, letters of recommendations and references from financial institutions.

Sasson and Salim erupted into nervous laughter as they filed the letter.

One day a Christian man came to Salim's wicket at the bank.

"Salim Abdullah?"

"Yes."

"I'm going to give you a piece of my mind," he said in a booming voice.

"What do you mean?"

"I'm Martel cognac broker and you offered their company your services."

"I've no idea what you're talking about."

"Buddy, don't pretend that butter wouldn't melt in your mouth. I got the lowdown on the Middle East Trading Bureau."

"Never heard of it," Salim said with a lump in his throat.

"Well, I'm telling you, kid – watch out! If anyone wants cognac, I'll handle their orders. A word to the wise: stay off my turf."

Although busy with a customer, Sasson witnessed the whole scene. A little later he told Salim: "Don't worry. We're out of here in a few months."

Salim wanted at all costs to avoid a scandal. That evening along the riverbank he voiced his concerns to Sasson who was busy partying. He'd just made his first sale: 1– extra large yashmaghs, Iraqi headdresses made of cotton in India. A barely literate Muslim merchant in Kut had ordered them.

"We can't collect our commission until they're delivered," Salim said.

"So what? It's just the beginning. We'll get more orders."

The bank had an endless list of foreign suppliers and local buyers.

"Within six months," Sasson said, "the word will spread so that we won't need to hunt up customers. For the time being only making a commission on sales will have to do."

After the Kut order others came from Kadhimain, Basra and even Saudi Arabia. Unlike most businesses who imported goods and sold them at a higher price, the Middle East Trading Bureau acted merely as brokers. They could hardly do otherwise since they had no capital.

It proved a red-letter day when Sasson and Salim received 60 dinars for their first commission. It amounted to more than two months of their combined salaries. They'd found a goose that would lay golden eggs. No paltry income, mean standard of living, or routine existence awaited them. Their gamble had paid off and they intended to push their luck. Salim normally proceeded with caution but now nothing could hold him back. In fact his ambitions and plans now surpassed Sasson to whom he proposed a night on the town. First they went to el Rafidaine, a new cabaret near the Al Zawraa movie theatre. This nightclub featured the best musicians from Egypt. Inaugurated by the sensational songstress, Umm Kulthum, the club's line-up thereafter included a who's who of male and female singers made popular by the radio. This new invention had found its way into all the big cafés.

That evening a Lebanese songstress, Asmahan, took the stage. Salim and Sasson arrived early, at nine o'clock, and ordered whiskey while the house band showcased its own musicians. Never before had Salim and Sasson drunk whiskey, much less go to this swanky cabaret. There they wouldn't be caught dead ordering arak, the lowly drink of local natives. However, whiskey, the Englishman's alcoholic beverage, didn't taste good to Salim and Sasson, though they wouldn't admit it.

The club featured a mix of sheikhs and tribal leaders sporting headdresses, but the audience consisted mostly of white collar workers in business suits.

When Asmahan appeared on stage, the drunken, impatient crowd wildly cheered her. Dainty, smiling and draped in a black, flowing cocktail dress, she strode confidently to the front. She had large brown eyes, a beauty mark on her cheek, and a somewhat longish face.

"Do you think she's pretty?" Sasson asked after a while.

"Not sure, but she has a beautiful voice."

Known for her chops, she could hold a high note for over a minute. Salim shut his eyes and floated on the waves of her voice.

The room burst into applause and there were shouts of Allah, Allah!

"Wake up!" Sasson exclaimed.

"Listen carefully, Sasson. It's sublime."

When Asmahan walked off stage well past midnight, the crowd went wild shouting, screaming and at times howling bawdily. Eventually, the club emptied except for a few who stayed glued to their seats and ordered bottles of arak.

"Are you crazy?" Sasson said. "We've just had the appetizer. Now we can enjoy the main course. Nadia's waiting for us."

Sasson had counted on the element of surprise. Nadia worked as a nurse's aide at the hospital until midnight. To supplement her income she served as a courtesan for select, reputable men. She didn't work in a brothel or with a pimp, so one couldn't consider her a common prostitute per se. Nadia's patrons normally didn't share her with others, but a client generously recommended Sasson to her. Nadia's guest of honour spent a night with her. It's true they paid, though that hardly mattered. A family in the Akoulia neighbourhood had agreed for a tidy sum to rent her a room where she could secretly entertain men. The neighbourhood had no whorehouses.

"She doesn't work tomorrow so we can have her all night."

This didn't represent their first visit to prostitutes but it did mark the first time they went together.

"How much?" Salim asked.

"One dinar each."

"She charges top dollar. Dancers earn that much."

"Nadia's not a prostitute. Besides, we're celebrating tonight. We can afford her."

As previously arranged, they quietly knocked three times at her door.

The door opened and a ray of light shot through the crack into the pitch black darkness that enveloped the house. They could barely see the face of the man who led them to Nadia. She was sitting in a room with all the curtains drawn. It had three wooden chairs and a table with a pitcher of water and yesterday's newspaper lying on it.

"Nadia, this is my friend Salim," Sasson said nonchalantly.

Olive-skinned, raven-haired, with small inky eyes, Nadia put no make-up on to cover the scar that disfigured her aquiline nose. She wore a pearl necklace to go with her red and white, striped, cotton dress. Sasson couldn't pass her off as a beauty queen, but then again she didn't look like a dog either. Salim would surely admit that. Small and thin, Nadia rose from the chair. Her breasts protruded from her tight dress.

"Who's coming first?" she asked, not bothering to beat about the bush.

"You go," Sasson said to Salim.

"No, you go."

Salim couldn't psych himself up for this. He didn't even want to. He had spent all day dreaming of a woman like Asmahan. He wanted to take a girl to the riverbank and speak with her for hours before making love. He'd never had a chance with Asmahan, yet her voice enchanted him. Now, without any transition time, he found himself in a prostitute's boudoir. What a comedown. However, he'd crossed the point of no return and couldn't simply go home and sleep.

Party time. They'd just taken their first steps on the road to fortune.

Nadia opened the door and Salim glimpsed a low bed, a basin, and a large jug. "Just like at the entrance of a mosque," he told himself. She grabbed Sasson and drew him into the bedroom. Red as a beet, he looked straight at Salim who kept his eyes glued to the floor.

"You can read the newspaper while waiting," Sasson said, guffawing.

Salim futilely tried to read the headlines amid the din of Sasson's nervous laughter in the next room. Sad and skittish he moved to another chair and started again to read. It didn't help because now Nadia's grating laughter added to the seemingly obscene cacophony. He opened the door into the dark hallway. Nadia's staccato voice stopped him in his tracks. A man doesn't run away. He shut out her naked body from of his mind, her mountainous breasts and lusty embrace of Sasson. He'd soon get his turn. Now, Salim couldn't wait to jump into that bed and lie naked with Nadia so as to feel a woman's bare flesh against his. But he felt ashamed of such lechery and despised himself for fucking the same hussy his friend had just screwed. Asmahan represented a true woman, one who remained beautiful and beyond reach. Nadia constituted nothing more than a prostitute who passed herself off as a nurse's aide to demand twice as much money. At the same time, he heard her laughing and wanted to squeeze her body tightly against his.

The door opened and Sasson came out grinning from ear to ear.

"She's waiting for you. Go on," he said. "Like the spider to the fly."

"Salim, I'm waiting for you," Nadia repeated, like a siren's song. Sasson pushed him into the room and closed the door.

Nadia sat on the bed in bikini panties and a bra. Her little-girl laugh contrasted sharply with her near total nudity and enticing, outstretched arms.

"Darling, you'll love me. Undress quickly."

Though not a prostitute, she spoke their language.

Salim removed his jacket, shirt and trousers, but not his underwear.

"If you show me yours I'll show you mine," she said.

She massaged his penis through his underwear.

"I'm a nurse," she whispered while removing his underwear. "I'm going to give this magnificent cock the treatment it deserves. When a man has such a handsome cock he must not hide it."

She unfastened her bra.

"Don't you want to see them?"

Salim threw himself on her, pulled down her panties and buried his face between her breasts.

"Wait, my darling. Your cock can't land without a parachute or it will get hurt."

She brought out a condom from underneath the pillow and with one hand deftly put it on his penis while she continued to massage it with her other hand.

"You're so handsome and clever."

He placed his lips against hers which she opened in order to slide her tongue into his mouth. Her breath reeked of onion but Salim repressed his disgust. He fondled her thighs, sucked her breasts, and it ended before it began. He had barely made eye contact with Nadia. Crestfallen and disappointed, he wanted the moment to last so that he could feel this woman's body against his. He wanted her so much, but it had already come to an end. She got up.

"Wait," he said.

"Darling, you can't start over."

"No. I'll come back, but right now I want to look at you naked."

Breasts, thighs, belly, Nadia stood there smelling of sweat and onions. Salim hadn't just imagined her. He lusted for her and felt he always would.

THE ORDERS KEPT FLOWING in: chemical dyes from Germany, leather purses from England, dolls from France, sweaters from Palestine.

One evening in their office, Sasson blurted out from sheer exhaustion: "We can't keep doing this. We work every night and don't even have time to take a walk. One of us must leave the bank."

"Why not both of us at the same time?"

"Not yet, Salim," Sasson said in a sagacious tone of voice. "We still need addresses, price lists, you know ..."

"Ok, then I'll quit. You're better at snooping around files in which you have no business."

This happened at the beginning of summer. The evening breeze caressed the air. People moved their beds onto rooftops and cosily snuggled under blankets so that only their faces felt the chill of early mornings. The sun would soon rise even earlier and then nobody would have the luxury of staying in bed.

Now that Salim had become his own boss, he went to the office at the warehouse between eight and nine o'clock in the morning, whereas at the bank he had to show up around seven o'clock.

Since becoming an importer he made a point of reading daily the *Iraq Times*, an English evening newspaper. One morning, while reading the previous day's issue alone on the roof, Salim heard from the neighbour's rooftop a voice singing a tune by the new Egyptian star, Layla Mourad. She played opposite Mohammed Abdul Wahab in films that Iraqis watched five, six, even ten times in order to hear these two singers. Word had it that she was Jewish and that her father served as cantor in a Cairo synagogue. The Jewish community proudly declared her an illustrious star and one of their own, but hesitated to admit that this cantor's daughter performed, and surely slept, with a Muslim. Salim froze. The voice echoed Asmahan's breathing and intonations but not as high-pitched. What a full-bodied voice, rich in the lower register yet achingly fragile.

If Salim had stood on the bed, he could have seen the singer on the other side of the wall that separated their homes. But he would certainly have frightened her and she would have stopped singing. He heard her fluffing the pillows as she made the beds.

"Who are the new neighbours?" he asked his mother.

"We don't know them. They're the Aghas from Basra. No one seems to know who they are but they seem an honourable family."

"How many are they?"

"Six. A man who just opened a grocery store at Taht el Takia, his wife, and their four children."

"Older children?"

"No, six years or younger."

"Do they have a maid?"

"You're suddenly very curious," she said warily.

"So what?"

"No. They're not wealthy enough to have a maid. They're caring for an 18-year-old niece. She's apparently an orphan, but since they're not from around here there's no way to verify this."

Every morning Salim lingered on the roof to keep a lookout for the neighbour. She sometimes sang so softly that he could barely hear her. Occasionally she stayed silent, but most often she sang Abdul Wahab, Farid Al Attrache, and Layla Mourad tunes. One day Salim heard the lady of the house call out: "Farida." He finally knew her name. She was beautiful, of that he had no doubt, even though he had never laid eyes on her. He tried to find a way to see her without scaring her away. The toilets remained open at the top. Standing on a toilet seat Salim could peer over the dividing wall on the stairwell side. He waited for her to finish tidying up. From his crow's-nest he saw only her hair, back, arms and legs. He knew that, like hundreds of other women, she had bronze skin and black hair – except that Farida was beyond doubt the most beautiful of them all.

Salim stood watch for her. Towards the end of the afternoon, he sat on a chair near his front door to read the newspaper. Or so he claimed. However, the few times that Farida left her house, she went out completely veiled. He could only see her graceful ankles. But at least that enabled him to distinguish her from her solidly-built aunt.

Each time he left or returned home, Salim thought of nothing but catching sight of Farida. One afternoon, coming home late for lunch, he noticed the neighbour's open door and walked slowly past it. There stood Farida without a veil. He stopped, smiled, tried but failed to utter a few words, then smiled again. Farida didn't rush to close the door. Salim believed he even espied the hint of a smile and her lips moving.

The heat proved unbearable. A blazing wind scorched his face. Sweat streamed down his neck and armpits. But he couldn't contain his joy. Farida was beautiful. Had he really seen her? She looked as beautiful as in his wildest dreams about her. What a smile! To top it off she recognized him and knew that he loved her. How could she not know? He had to wait two days before hearing her sing on the rooftop. My darling, the love of my heart. Thus she answered his call.

A week later Salim came home at the same time in the afternoon. His heart pounded wildly. Farida had left the door open and stood there waiting for him. He scarcely muttered: "Farida." She smiled and slowly went inside. He had no doubts this time. She too kept watching for him. He dared not believe it but now had the certainty that she loved him. How could she not love him?

He planned his day around her. In the morning she sang for him and when he came home in the afternoon she stood in the doorway. On the days he regularly came home early, he saw her looking out the window. After a while he understood. She couldn't come to the door until the whole family, including the children, fell fast asleep. At siesta time no one walked the burning streets. However, if somebody happened to pass by, Farida hid behind the door without completely shutting it.

Love gave Salim wings so that he had boundless energy and worked furiously. Every time he sealed a deal he knew how proud it would make Farida and that she would say to him what no other woman had ever said to a man. He often was on the verge of revealing this to Sasson with whom he wanted to share his joy. But not while Sasson complained about the bank and the gruelling hours he put in there.

"I'm working more than you," Sasson said.

"I know but you're working for yourself so there's no comparison."

Sasson expected him to suggest that he resign from the bank but Salim carefully avoided this. Salim feared Sasson might then interrupt his daily morning "dates" with Farida.

Once a week Sasson spent the night with Nadia. She met up him at the end of the afternoon. He brought bread, cheese, fruits, pastries, and a quart of arak. Nadia enjoyed drinking. They no longer met at midnight. She claimed to feel exhausted after working her shift though perhaps it was because she had other friends, even if she denied it. Nadia stopped counting the hours she spent with Sasson and he stopped counting how much money he gave her.

"Nadia always asks about you," he told Salim.

"I'd sure like to see her again."

"I'll tell her that. I don't think she's going with anyone else."

Salim wondered if Sasson had become jealous. How foolish – over a prostitute no less. Yet Salim thought it best not to press the point.

The next day Sasson welcomed him with a big smile and these words: "Nadia spoke about you to a girlfriend. She's waiting for you at eight o'clock tonight at the Akoulia house."

"But I ...," Salim said in protest, having been caught by surprise.

"Do you suddenly have trouble getting it up? You can't spend your life at that warehouse."

If Sasson only knew!

"What's her name?" Salim asked.

"Nouriah."

"Tonight, Nouriah will get all the love a man can give a woman. I hope she expects nothing less."

"No," Sasson said, playing along with the game. "She knows you're aware of her face."

"Too bad we have to talk about that."

"Yes, it's a shame," Sasson sighed wistfully.

By the time he arrived at the Akoulia house, Salim no longer had any qualms. In fact, he enjoyed the charade of such liaisons.

To his surprise he didn't feel this betrayed his love for Farida. Rather, this would vicariously prove it to her.

WATER AND PREVIOUS DAY'S *Al Zaman*. "They only buy day-old newspapers," Salim jokingly said to himself.

Nouriah opened the door. She had already removed her veil. She had fair, so-called flaxen-coloured skin, brown eyes, a large mouth, a long pointed nose, and brown hair cut short like women from the West.

"I'm thirsty," she said. "I hurried here."

Salim recognized her Christian accent, perhaps Armenian or from Mosul in the north.

He shook her hand.

"You look just the way Nadia described you," he said. "Do you also work at the hospital?"

"Yes," she answered, hesitantly.

"You're prettier than Nadia's description."

Her lack of response indicated she probably hadn't understood.

He drew her close to himself.

"I mean you're beautiful," he said with conviction.

"And you're handsome."

She came across as less brazen than Nadia. Perhaps she wasn't as experienced and hadn't yet learned the ropes. He led her into the room and next to the bed.

"Get undressed."

She smiled sadly then took off her white blouse with blue embroidery and her pink skirt. She wore a petticoat which she slowly, if not reluctantly, removed as though she was having second thoughts about it. Salim already stood naked. He threw her on the bed and began kissing her. She smelt of rose water and powder.

"You know," she said, "I don't ..."

She stopped talking and started in turn to kiss him.

He kept seeing Farida's face. He closed his eyes and there she lay beside him, completely naked, and he passionately penetrated her. He'd waited so long for this moment. Although stiff at first, Nouriah relaxed and soon wrapped her arms around Salim. He almost cried out, "Farida," but suddenly anger overwhelmed and paralyzed him. He moved away from Nouriah. The sweaty smell of her armpits' black tufts intoxicated him. She had a solid build with strong, muscular thighs.

Did her presence in his life reduce Farida to a prostitute also? He had to cleanse the honour of the love of his life. One day Farida too would lie on the bed waiting for him and he would love her and belong to her. He felt Nouriah's unsure, clumsy hand on him. Neither he, nor she, nor Farida, had much experience caressing. He resented her for not being Farida. He again mounted her, putting the full weight of his body on hers. But this time he gently, tenderly penetrated her as though to ask forgiveness for previously mistreating her. He would henceforth love and caress all the women of the world because he loved Farida and belonged to her just as she belonged to him body and soul.

Nouriah got up, crouched in front of the water basin, and started to wash herself. Unlike Nadia, she hadn't asked Salim to clean his penis before getting in bed with her. He stood next to Nouriah and also began to wipe away the many diseases he might have contracted in that moment of passion. He had no right to contaminate his body since it no longer belonged to him. He couldn't do that to Farida.

His eye caught Nouriah's bittersweet, pleading look. She wanted ... How stupid of him to forget she's a prostitute. Contrary to Sasson, he would pay her in full. He stretched out his arm to touch her and help her to towel down but instantly changed his mind and instead tickled her stomach and underarms. She laughed uninhibitedly like a child, without flirtatiousness nor crassness. She laughed full of joy and satisfaction.

They stood there naked. Embarrassed, Salim glanced away. He had always paid to see a woman naked yet he didn't hold it against Nouriah for being a ... He dressed quickly, pulled a dinar out of his wallet, folded the bill and slipped it into her hand. Without looking at it, she put it in her purse. Salim then took a half-dinar bill out of his wallet and stuffed that too in her purse. This didn't constitute excessive generosity. He thus redeemed himself for treating her as a hired prostitute and apologized to Farida for making love to her from afar and through an intermediary which nevertheless enabled him to love her with his whole body and not just in a dream.

They got ready to leave and Salim opened the door for Nouriah but she stood still, unmoving.

What had happened between them? She amounted to nothing more than a prostitute and he had paid her more than enough.

"If I want to see you again ...," he said.

"Whenever you want ..."

His face lit up.

"How? Through Nadia?"

"If you want …"

"Can't I …?"

Would he have to tell Sasson, go through Nadia, and shout it from the rooftops each time he wanted to have sex?

"Where can I reach you? At the hospital?"

"No, better not to."

Salim had known all along that she didn't work at the hospital. She gave him an address at Bab el Charqui. He simply needed to leave a blank piece of paper with the letter "S" on the day before he wanted to see her. They would always meet at eight o'clock in the evening at the same address.

"Could you come any day of the week?" he asked.

"Yes."

"Do you live there?"

"No. I'm a private nurse … I work …"

Salim dropped the matter. Perhaps she worked as a house servant or a kind of maid.

"So did you find Nouriah pretty?" Sasson asked him the next day.

"Not bad. Compared to Nadia …"

He wanted to make Sasson feel good, or to at least not hurt his feelings.

At times he seemed so distant and infuriating to Salim. They talked a lot about what their business needed: a second typewriter, another table, maybe a secretary? If so they would have to move.

"There's an office at the el Khedhairi warehouse," Sasson said.

He took care of everything and just kept Salim in the loop.

"We're in good shape here," Salim said.

"We've placed enough orders that we can …"

"We have all we need here."

Yet Salim remained edgy, bad tempered, and above all unhappy. Sasson decided not to press the point. He walked Salim home and they talked only about Nadia and Nouriah the whole way.

"Guess what? Someday we will rent a little house far from here, in Elwiyah, Karradah, or the Slekh. There no one knows us and we won't need to go anymore to the Akoulia district."

Salim calmed down.

"Sasson, you've always got great ideas," he said cheerfully.

He would have the house to himself two or three days a week and he could use it as he saw fit.

THAT DAY PROVED A SCORCHER and the wind lashed them at dusk.

"Would you like to take a stroll?" Sasson asked.

"I'm too tired."

Salim's mother sat in the entryway and gave Sasson an unexpectedly warm welcome.

"Sit down," she said as she got up. "I'll bring a couple of chairs."

Salim wondered if he should feel thankful or embarrassed about this.

"Don't hurry off, Sasson," Salim's mother said. "It's still light out. Because of you I get to see my son before going to sleep."

Thanks to the clack of her wooden *kabkab* shoes on the tiles, they heard Najiah coming. She wore a flowery dress and pinned back her hair with a comb. She walked carefully carrying a tray with four glasses filled with orangeade. Sasson couldn't keep his eyes off her but, when Salim stared him down, he looked at the floor.

"You're going out of your way for us."

"In this heat I spend my day drinking," Salim's mother said.

With a big smile Najiah put the tray on the ground and then sipped her orangeade standing up.

"Would you like to sit down?" Sasson asked, rising from his seat.

She turned her head slightly from right to left to say no.

"She never stops," her mother said. "She sews, knits, and cooks, besides reading constantly. She'll wear out her eyes with all those books. What does she see in them? Before you know it I'll have nothing left to do in this house. If they don't kick me out of it first."

"Your business partner's quite the gentleman," Salim's mother said after Sasson had gone. "He's polite and considerate. Although not a prominent family, the Karkouklis have a spotless reputation. There is no family history of mental illness, tuberculosis, or promiscuity. Does he drink?"

"No and he doesn't bet on horses or gamble at the poker tables. He seems to interest you."

"We're just talking. That doesn't hurt anybody."

To his own astonishment Salim felt glad about conniving with his mother. He divined her scheme and had no objections to it. He also saw no contradiction between considering Sasson a future brother-in-law and renting a house where both of them could host Nadia, Nouriah, and other women.

"It surprised me that you willingly let Najiah meet an unknown man, indeed a stranger," he said.

Salim's mother didn't realize that he meant to tease her. They hardly ever spoke because Naji got all the attention.

"He's not a stranger," Najiah said. "He's your business partner whom you talk about night and day."

Salim laughed heartily.

"Sasson's a good boy and a gentleman."

Salim retired early and didn't hear a peep from his neighbour's rooftop. They always went to bed at dusk. The father rose at dawn and awoke the rest of the family. Was Farida sleeping and dreaming of him? He slid his hand under the pillow to touch the note he would give her the next morning. He couldn't sleep so he turned onto his back and sought to count the stars. This somehow made him feel closer to Farida and his goals. But which ones? He skirted the question and yet it troubled him.

Salim heard Farida's voice and the sound of her putting away the mattresses to protect them from the sun. He hoisted himself up the separating wall and tapped the top of it with his hand. Farida gingerly approached and his heart skipped a beat when he glimpsed her unveiled beauty. He signalled to her by waving the note in his hand.

He threw the folded piece of paper over the fence, smiled, and climbed down from his perch without uttering a word, although he had intended to do so. In his head he had repeated a hundred times the first sentence he would say to her. On the piece of paper he wrote only this: "Farida, I love you. Salim." He then suddenly panicked. What if she was illiterate and couldn't read? He dismissed the idea as impossible because he loved her.

When he came home that afternoon, he saw Farida's radiant face smiling behind her door. She whispered: "Salim," and then fell silent. At the sight of a veiled woman coming around the corner, he walked right past the door as though he had heard nothing.

Farida sang earlier than usual the next morning. It amazed Salim and he wondered if she realized that she surpassed all other singers in the world. He didn't immediately respond out of fear that she was not alone. Farida sang: "*Yo habibi*, my love." While waiting for him to climb to the top of the wall, she folded the mattresses and stored them under a trellis, in the shade. He threw over his note: "Farida, I worship you. I love you. I adore your singing. Salim." She walked towards him, raised her arm and beckoned him to take the piece of paper she held in her hand. They froze on the spot and stared at one another.

"Farida," he stammered.

She placed her index finger on his lips then backed away. On grade school paper, with childlike handwriting, she had scribbled in pencil: "Salim, I love you too. Farida." After reading, re-reading, and sniffing her note, he carefully put it in his wallet amid the money bills.

That afternoon Salim found the neighbours' front door closed. He turned white as a sheet. Had they discovered his messages? He should have advised Farida that she could tear them up if she needed to. He shouldn't have written her name nor his. He got mad at himself. Yet how could he not mention the name that meant everything to him? He walked past Farida's door, around the block, and then back to her house. The door stayed tightly shut. Like it or not he kept on walking. Sweat soaked the front, back and sleeves of his shirt. The heat consumed Salim and gave him a pounding headache. He wanted to throw himself on their doorstep and wail. Everything had fallen into ruin. Would he never again see Farida? Perhaps they had shipped her back home. Maybe they had locked her up.

He walked slowly past the door a third time and it opened. Farida stood there with a child in her arms. "Sleep my sweetheart, sleep my beloved," she sang while looking straight into Salim's eyes as he walked by.

Her words gave him wings and he floated on cloud nine all the way home. There he undressed and lay on the sofa.

"Eat before you fall asleep," his mother said.

Famished, he got up, wolfed down his meal, and then took a long nap. At the end of the afternoon, Najiah awakened him.

"Sasson's at the door. He wants to talk to you."

As he washed his face and put on a clean shirt, he heard his mother say: "Come on in, Sasson. Don't stay outside. You're at home here."

Salim found Sasson in the courtyard sitting on the edge of a chair and eyeing his sister who sat knitting at the opposite end of the courtyard.

"I'm sorry for coming to your house," Sasson said.

"No problem. Najiah, did you offer Sasson something to drink?"

She didn't answer him but instantly got up and went into the kitchen.

"Don't bother," Sasson said. "I can't stay and only came because this evening I'll arrive at the office after you've left so I wanted to remind you that tomorrow we must sign the lease for the el Khedhairi building, unless ..."

"Count me in. Does tomorrow at five work for you?"

"We have to let them know."

"I'll drop over tomorrow morning before going to the office."

Najiah came back with two glasses of orangeade. Had she surreptitiously put on lipstick?

Sasson felt more at ease and said: "You must find it hard to knit in this heat!"

"It's cotton," Najiah said, as she scurried away.

Sasson left immediately.

The next morning Farida sang: "*Ya laili, Ya aini* (Oh night, Oh starlit eyes)." Salim cast his note over the wall: "Farida, my love. I think about you day and night. Salim."

She in turn threw her piece of paper which twirled through the air. They looked at each other and Farida again sang: "*Ya laili, Ya aini.*" She sang sublimely and improvised like a virtuoso to boot.

He read her message. "Salim, my love. Tomorrow, three o'clock, at El Saadoun Park."

He couldn't contain his joy.

At last he would have the chance to talk with, and maybe even touch her. How clever of her to choose El Saadoun Park in mid-afternoon when no one went there because of the heat. How judicious of her to avoid Ghazi Park with its crowds.

In his excitement Salim decided to walk to the office despite the heat. His mood darkened while walking. Was he the first and only man in Farida's life? After all, she had taken the initiative to meet and had chosen both the time and place. Perhaps she regularly did this, although he convinced himself otherwise. She loved him and that love made her creative. What about him? Why hadn't he thought of arranging a meeting?

He lacked style, savvy, and guts. But the thought of meeting up with Farida dispelled all his fears and filled him with joy and courage rather than doubt.

The next day he went home early for lunch. He took his time in the shower and put on a clean shirt.

"I'm going to the office," he declared.

"At this hour?" Najiah asked.

Was that a taunting smile on her face? Did she know about his rendezvous? Maybe from the courtyard Najiah had espied him on the wall exchanging notes with Farida. Their secret would soon get out. His face radiated love for Farida. He wanted to tell everyone: Farida's the greatest singer and the most beautiful woman in the world.

Salim arrived at the park after carefully pacing himself so that Farida would not see him exhausted, his shirt blotched with sweat and his face turning purple. The sun beat down on the vegetation and blanched it. Even the roses seemed white. He sought shade to escape his enemy, the omnipresent sun that mercilessly pursued him through the streets. He heard birds in the park but it appeared otherwise deserted. He had the entire park to himself. He looked for a tree big enough to shelter him yet quickly left it out of concern that Farida might not see him. He darted from one tree to another, never content with his position. The sun melted the asphalt of the traffic circle while he kept looking for a friendly tree.

A veiled woman holding a basket came towards him. It couldn't be Farida since this old woman shuffled along, and besides Farida wouldn't bring a basket. Nonetheless, the woman slowly approached him. He stood still in the burning sun and checked his watch: ten minutes past three. Perhaps Farida got tied up? He'd see her the next day. Henceforth, love would bind them together, and nobody could keep them apart. The woman crossed in front of him and whispered: "Salim." It sounded like heavenly music to his ear.

"Let's go in the shade," she said.

He wanted to speak, to say something but choked on the words as if they had stuck in his windpipe. No one could recognize Farida because of her veil and as a man he needn't worry. Men had the right to appear in public with a woman, whether their sister, mother or, he thought to himself, a prostitute, though that word upset him. They stopped behind a tree.

"Farida."

He wanted to add but found it impossible to say out loud: "My love, my sweetheart."

"Salim."

In the end she, not he, broke the grip of silent emotions.

"I told them we're out of sesame oil. Tomorrow it's *tich beab* and we must prepare the date pudding. My aunt's taking care of the children's afternoon nap and her husband sleeps like a log. I'll tell them that I had to go a good distance to find a grocery store that was open."

At first she spoke quickly but then less hurriedly. He listened to her voice without paying attention to the words. He'd waited so long for this moment and had constantly dreamt of it. Yet now she stood there talking about sesame oil. Her voice possessed the melodious quality of music.

"I left the office early," he said. "I had a business appointment this afternoon that I rescheduled for tomorrow. I changed shirts."

"I'm so happy you could come."

"I would have dropped everything and done anything to be near you. I'm not making this up, Farida. I think about you day and night."

She didn't respond. She amounted to a bundle of black cloth with no eyes, mouth, or body. He would have given anything to touch her, hold her hands, and look into her eyes. He felt his entire body quiver in her presence, at being so close to her.

"I can't stop thinking about you," he repeated.

While he lay in bed, he visualized speaking passionately with her, revealing his deepest feelings. But now he couldn't find the words to tell her how much he loved her.

He imagined that underneath the veil she was smiling and quite emotional. They walked to an area shaded by two trees and, once they knew no one could see them, she lifted her veil. Her eyes flashed. Salim said to himself that never before had he seen a woman, a true woman. His sister and mother didn't count, and Nouriah even less.

"Farida," he blurted out. Even as he said it, he thought it stupid that he got no further than saying over and over: "Farida, Farida."

"Salim."

"I adore hearing you say my name. It's one of your most beautiful songs."

"Do you enjoy my songs?"

"You're the best singer in the whole world."

"I love singing."

"I can no longer live without hearing you sing. I can't go on living without you."

"I so wanted to hear you say that," she said, in tears. "I've dreamt of you telling me this."

"I talk to you every waking moment – at the office, in the street, on the roof."

"I do the same with you."

Did their meeting have a specific purpose? A reason? He wanted to ask Farida but feared this would offend her so he didn't bring it up. By coming to him she ran enormous risks whereas he had nothing to lose. If he seduced a girl, that would only prove his manliness. Indeed Sasson would give him a slap on the back and say: "Way to go, Salim." It would make him a champ, if not a hero.

On the other hand, it would make her a prostitute. To remove her veil and unashamedly present herself to a man meant embarking on a perilous path that endangered her future. Farida's life would forever change. This made Salim love her even more. He would never forsake her. Though she would be considered a fallen woman, he would not lapse into pity for her. No, he would always assume his responsibility as her man.

"I have to leave now," she said.

"Why?"

"They'll start to get suspicious."

She stood up. Salim was about to follow her.

FARIDA

"Don't walk with me, Salim. People will recognize you."

He did an about-face away from her and, at the traffic circle, eagerly stepped right into the fiery furnace of the midday sun. He wanted it to liquefy and absorb him. With proof that he loved Farida and that she loved him, he considered himself the world's richest, most powerful man.

Sweat covered his body. He quenched his thirst at Bab el Charqui with a soda pop which he drank in the shade of Ghazi Park. The afternoon wind scorched his face.

One by one he went over Farida's last words. "Don't walk with me, Salim. People will recognize you." Her voice had sounded gentle yet firm. She had thought of everything. He didn't know whether to admire her for this or to let everyone in on their secret.

ALTHOUGH HE HADN'T YET set a specific date, Sasson decided to quit his job at the bank at the end of summer.

"We're now well established," he said.

They no longer needed the secret information from the bank and his salary paled in comparison to their bank deposits. Small wonder Sasson had proposed drawing up the necessary paperwork to legalize their business. Without regard for cost they also brightly furnished the new office in the el Khedhairi building.

Sasson used every excuse in the book to stop by Salim's house. Najiah and her mother must have realized this because they always met him at the door, invited him in, and offered him something to drink. Najiah hastily put on lipstick and dolled herself up. She looked pretty to Salim. Her mother made no secret of her hope that Sasson would ask for Najiah's hand in marriage. The answers to her queries convinced Najiah's mother that Sasson came from a respectable albeit modest family that had no history of hereditary disease or prostitution. Since the Abdullah family enjoyed a higher social status, Sasson would not demand a dowry nor its trappings.

Najiah's good looks alone justified this. She would enter into the marriage with at most a trousseau that included clothes but no silverware or furniture. If Sasson unduly delayed proposing marriage, the Abdullah family would have someone act as a mediator. Their father proved useless in such matters because he spent his days lost in prayer and, as Sasson's business partner, Salim couldn't broach the subject.

Sasson kept a lookout for the best opportunity to officially launch their business. They would soon no longer simply serve as sales representatives who only received a commission. Instead, they would become genuine import/export brokers who not only earned commissions but also turned a profit.

Sasson didn't breathe a word to Nadia about his visits to the Abdullahs yet Salim knew that he saw her two or three times a week. If he wanted to marry Najiah, he'd have to control himself and call less frequently on Nadia. Salim wouldn't preach to Sasson but, as Najiah's brother, he couldn't completely shut his eyes to this.

On some mornings, Farida sang coded messages. She chose Asma or Abdul Wahab's pop songs but replaced their lyrics with hers. Salim thus learned, for instance, that one of the children had to remain in bed and this meant she couldn't go out of the house. They still passed each other messages over the wall and she continued to pen them in her schoolgirl handwriting. "My sweetheart, I love you. I'm thinking of you." Salim had too many for his wallet and consequently put a dozen in-between the pages of a poetry book. What if Najiah fancied poking her nose in it? Salim decided what he'd do. If ever his secret got out, he would announce that he intended to ask for Farida's hand in marriage. They couldn't refuse them.

"Tomorrow, three o'clock at Ghazi Park. Farida." This put her at risk. Did she do this on purpose?

He recognized her by her shoes.

"I can't stay very long and it's too far to El Saadoun Park," she said.

"I want to talk to you and look at you without the veil."

"I do too."

"I thought of reserving box seats for the afternoon film at Al Zawraa cinema in the Sinak neighbourhood," he said.

"The Al Hamraa cinema's better because only Muslims go there."

In box seats no one would see them anyway, but he didn't want to argue.

"Tomorrow?"

"Out of the question," she said. "I'll tell you when."

"You don't have much time."

"I can't wait to leave that family. They claim to have saved my life. I was happy at Hilla. We're poor but we love each other. My mother didn't discriminate between sons and daughters. She gave them the same food and the same portions. My dear father earns a pittance as an accountant and my aunt despises her brother for it. She swears by her husband who's an uncouth idiot, and a cheat on top of it. He tricks customers by always smiling at them while he uses fake weights and measures. He entices them with dainties such as dried fruit for adults and candy for children."

"What about you?" he asked.

"Me? The family kept me out of school to serve as their unpaid maid. My aunt teaches me cooking and sewing to prepare me for marriage. But who'll marry me without a dowry?"

"I will," Salim replied with exuberance.

She stopped talking and started to cry.

"Farida, I love you and don't need a dowry. Besides, you're the most beautiful woman in the world. How dare anyone ask for a dowry?"

Muslim children, barefoot and their legs covered with mud, scurried around Salim and Farida. The children ran up to the column of water that the fountain sprayed and then hurried back into the sunshine.

Jasmine no longer bloomed but the scent of roses filled the air.

"What will your family say?" Farida asked.

"You'll become my wife. I alone make that decision."

"Salim, we're not living in a Hollywood movie."

"You don't want to get married?"

Her refusal hurt him and he almost blew up.

"Salim, if you only knew how much I think about you! I give myself to you forever."

Tears welled up in his eyes. What would she think of a man who cries? He stifled the tears. If he could just see her. For the time being his life came down to a bundle of black cloth, a silhouette in the sun.

"You don't think about me anymore," Nouriah complained while she unbuttoned her blouse.

"I'm here."

In the bed Salim fiercely seized hold of her to somehow avenge Farida whose image he nevertheless shunned. By pulling Nouriah tightly to himself, he sought simultaneously to pay tribute to Farida and to put her out of his mind. Even though he held Nouriah in his arms, Salim remained faithful to Farida. For him she represented life, as his bursts of passion demonstrated.

"Nadia told me that you and Sasson will rent a house at Karradah."

He knew nothing about this but masked his surprise.

"It's not a done deal."

"Salim, you've nothing to fear from me. You know, I'm not what you think. You're the only …"

Nouriah still lay naked and dripping with sweat next to him. Leaning on his elbow he licked her breasts and belly, causing her to giggle like a child.

"You're tickling me."

She put her arms around him.

"Nadia has already visited the house and you kept the secret from me …"

She morphed suddenly from a playful child into a demanding woman.

"Promise you'll take me there."

Salim kissed and nibbled Nouriah to make her stop talking.

"I don't like coming here. People will think I'm a call girl. It doesn't matter how much I repeat that you're the only ..."

Was she trying to entrap him? If so, what a burden. He didn't want any other woman. She served only as a stopgap for Farida, the woman for whom he waited. The whole situation confused him. There stood Nouriah in the flesh, unveiled, yet she seemed as invisible as the woman whose eyes alone shone through her black burka.

Nouriah too then completely draped herself in black so that she assumed the spectral form of a dark, elusive shadow. Salim slipped two dinars into her hand and she kissed him as a sign of forgiveness.

He felt dirty. Farida never ... Although in abeyance, his desire for her remained the anchor of his life.

SUMMER DREW TO A close. The cool evening breeze effaced the hot sun. Clouds appeared but quickly vanished. The first rain could catch by surprise people sleeping on their rooftops.

It enraged Salim that Sasson hadn't breathed a word to him about the rented house. How would he broach the subject with Sasson? He could already hear his partner's response: "I rented it for myself and don't answer to you." Yet didn't their partnership extend to everything? Be that as it may, Sasson knew nothing about Farida ...

The next day Sasson nonchalantly declared with a sly smile: "I rented a house at Karradah."

"Oh!" Salim said with feigned innocence. "Why? For Nadia?"

Sasson didn't pick up on the mixture of anger, disappointment and irony in Salim's voice.

"You can use the house, if you want."

"When?" Salim asked.

"Whenever you want ..."

"Not when Nadia ..."

"Why not? Nouriah's her friend. The four of us could have fun together."

"Have you already furnished the house?"

"Barely. Two large beds, chairs, tables and some pots and pans. I let Nadia take care of it."

Nadia's getting too big for her britches, Salim said to himself as he thought about his sister. But he half-heartedly concluded that it didn't matter in the end.

"We'll share the rent," he said.

"If you want."

"We should divvy up the week because I don't want to intrude when you wish to remain alone with Nadia."

"Salim, we normally work things out between us," Sasson said in a conciliatory tone. "We don't need to write down rules and regulations. If you want to have the house to yourself for a day or two, just give me a little advance notice."

ONE DAY IN SEPTEMBER they kicked off their new lives as rich, decadent bachelors. Although the heat had abated, it still held people in its grip.

To drum up passengers the driver of the small bus called out: "Ulwiyah, Karradah, Masbah." He couldn't turn a profit unless six or seven persons made the trip.

"When do we leave?" Sasson snapped.

"Immediately," the drive calmly responded as he continued to shout. "Karradah, Ulwiyah, Masbah."

They finally left Bab el Charqui and headed towards Ulwiyah.

Sasson and Salim remained the only passengers on the bus when it came to the last stop at Karradah, a vacant lot designated for a swimming pool. Sasson went ahead of Salim to show him the way. The house had a courtyard, three rooms, a kitchen and a shower. Acting like the master of the house, Sasson opened all its doors and awaited Salim's comments as he looked a room up and down. It had a bed, a bamboo armchair and a table and chairs. Some items of women's clothing hung from hooks on the wall while a man's pants and shirt lay on the bed. The room next to it appeared identical. Sasson waited in the doorway. Salim relaxed but had mixed emotions. On one hand, seeing all his friend had done deeply touched Salim. On the other hand, Sasson had kept him completely in the dark about this, which galled Salim to no end.

"It's your room," Sasson murmured somewhat sheepishly. "I furnished it just like mine. Salim, I had to act quickly because Nadia wouldn't see me and I couldn't wait any longer. This embarrassed me so much that I didn't want to talk about it with you. Someday you'll understand. In the meantime I'm begging you to share this house with me."

"But ..."

"I'll cover the expenses."

Sasson brought Salim into the kitchen which had more bamboo armchairs, a large table, pitchers and an ice chest.

"I'm very embarrassed, Salim. You're my brother. To lead a secret life and a house for ... You're the last person who should find out about this. One day you'll understand."

He had a half-conniving, half-pleading look. Then suddenly he smiled and said: "Salim, you're going to kill me. I have a surprise for you. Our two women will soon arrive. That's my surprise."

The moment Sasson turned to face him, Salim broke down and hugged him.

"You're my brother," Sasson said. "There's no house, no Nadia without you."

"You should have ..."

"Forget it, Salim. I guarantee you'll understand someday."

A knock sounded at the door.

"They're here," Sasson blurted out.

Two shadows, two bodies shrouded in black, appeared. They hesitated then timidly approached.

"Wow, what a big house," Nouriah exclaimed as she hung her veil on a hook.

After absorbing the surprise of it all, joy filled Salim. He hadn't realized that he could scarcely wait to see Nouriah again.

"Are you happy?" Sasson asked.

Overcome with emotion, Salim squeezed Sasson's shoulder. However, he didn't love Nouriah. In his longing he only desired her as a substitute for his true love.

Nadia acted like the mistress of the household. While busying herself in the kitchen, she gave orders to Nouriah for setting the table. The motions she went through reminded Salim of Najiah following their mother's orders. This calmed him and served as a diversion. He would never have believed that familiarity and desire went hand in hand. He associated a man's desire for a woman with secrets and intimations. But there Nadia stood, first wiping the table and then heartily eating a slice of watermelon whose seeds she spit into her hand and carefully piled on a corner of her plate.

"It's sweet," Nadia declared. "Sasson, you sure know how to pick a good watermelon."

She then turned towards Nouriah.

"Sasson knows how to do everything. He's a genius and a tiger."

After glancing at Sasson, Nouriah's eyes begged Salim to come to her rescue. She felt a stranger there. She needed him, a man, to show her the ropes around this place.

"You're wearing a pretty dress," Salim remarked.

"Isn't it though?" Nadia said. "She so feared that you wouldn't like this material. Didn't I tell you?" Nouriah went beet red. "We shopped together for fabrics at the bazaar. Sasson, what about my dress? Do you like it just as much?"

"Yes, when you put it on a hook in the wall."

Salim resented his friend's shameless vulgarity and later he would tell him so, but for the time being these women had come to do just that, namely, to take off their clothes. Yet Salim asked himself what right he had to go there when Farida …

While Nouriah washed the dishes, Sasson led Nadia into the bedroom and shut the door. Salim heard their bawdy laughter which soon gave way to silence. Feeling alternately disgusted and lustful, Salim slyly gazed at Nouriah. She kept busy wiping the table and folding the napkins. When she raised her arms to put dishes in the cupboard, a burst of sensuality shot through him and he thrust his body against her backside. She faced him, wrapped her arms around him, and started covering his forehead, neck and nose with little kisses. He let her do it while he waited to see ... Nouriah looked languishingly at him.

"She's not here for money," he said to himself, and wondered if he wouldn't have preferred that. She stopped necking and went to sit in a chair. It would have proven offensive, and unmanly, if he had not accepted her advances, much less pushed her away. What would Sasson have said? How would Salim explain Farida to him, the man who would soon ask for his sister's hand in marriage?

In the bedroom Salim hurriedly stripped Nouriah without even looking at her and then assailed her body. She held him tight and whispered so softly that he could only make out these words: "My love, my love." He got off her and she reached for the sheet to cover herself. But he stopped her so she put her hand over his eyes. Her contented smile exuded the happiness he brought her and in return for this sign of affection Salim caressed her thighs and abdomen and then he buried his face in her breasts.

The smell of sweat intoxicated him and he mounted her again bringing to bear the full weight of his body so that he almost crushed her. Yet she didn't complain; instead, she accepted this and, as soon as he let go of her, she again offered him her body, a body that called to him. "Nouriah, Nouriah," he said over and over. After a while the spectre of

Farida troubled Salim's soul. But he rejected these intrusive thoughts and resumed fondling Nouriah's breasts with his tongue until her sweat mingled with his.

Night fell and silence reigned except for Sasson's whispers, Nadia's muffled laughs and dogs barking in the distance.

"I must go home," Nouriah said with a sigh.

"The next time you'll stay overnight."

"Oh yes! All night."

Her eagerness both flattered and embarrassed Salim.

"I'll never forget you," she said.

"Nor will I ever forget you."

The next week he would claim that he had to make a trip to Basra or Kirkuk. He and Nouriah would spend all night alone and naked. She'd murmur repeatedly: "My love, my love, " and tell him: "I'll never forget you." Not to disappoint her he'd respond: "Nor will I ever forget you." But he'd say it reluctantly, without true feeling. After all, he'd already given his heart to the only woman …

By ten o'clock in the evening the women had dressed and prepared to put on their veils.

"The next time we'll spend the night together," Sasson said, echoing Salim. "We'll start with dinner, just like in the movies."

Nouriah looked at Salim for confirmation of this but he gave her the cold shoulder.

On the far horizon the big city slumbered, leaving them to do as they chose. An empty minibus was parked two streets away and, when the driver heard them, he immediately started calling out: "Bab el Charqui."

"I'll pay for five people if you go right now," Sasson said.

They drove in silence through the dark night. Cafés with a few customers dotted Bustan el Khass, a suburb of the city. In Bab el Charqui the two couples parted company.

At Sinak Nouriah whispered: "You can drop me off here. I live in the third house."

"Get a load of that," Salim said to himself. "She works for Jews. She must have told them her aunt lay dying ... Next time it's her uncle's turn on the deathbed." Salim wanted to hug Nouriah as a thank you for the lies she told on his account.

"I'll find a way to spend the night with you," she said in a low, stifled voice.

"I'll contact you."

AT THE END OF summer, when the morning air cooled, Salim lingered in bed. The sun rose slowly over the rooftop and he welcomed its rays. Farida had never sung more feelingly. He knew she sang for him. They exchanged notes but he put off the day for their date even though he had it all worked out in his mind. He seemed to fear this would sever a link that would end the quiet certainty of their love. Nevertheless, he finally wrote down his plan on one of their daily notes. Farida should let him know on which afternoon she could get away.

When he deciphered her child-like handwriting, the note read: "Tomorrow my darling. Your beloved." Salim's hands trembled. At the office that day he couldn't do any paperwork but instead kept drinking coffee.

He arrived a half-hour early and moviegoers already swarmed the theatre. He had gone there the day before to reserve a box for this matinee show. Salim chose the Al Hamraa theatre because it only screened Egyptian films and on weekdays in the afternoon only Muslims came so no one would recognize them and even if ...

He stood at the entrance scrutinizing the shoes worn by the veiled women. Could he identify Farida? Women entered two or three at a time. To avoid being jostled at the ticket booth, they paid boys to buy their tickets. Salim checked his pocket to make sure he had his ticket. Tired and thirsty, he decided he'd buy two bottles of soda pop at their theatre box. A woman walked alone in front of the movie house and did not stop.

"It's her," he said to himself.

He stepped outside as the woman turned and walked back. He couldn't very well go up to her without running the risk of mistaking another woman for Farida. And then in turn running the risk of having to answer to a husband or brother. He couldn't afford to take the chance.

"Salim," she whispered, solving his problem.

Farida followed him without saying another word. He showed his ticket and they entered the box. They had all four seats to themselves because he had reserved the entire box. In the neighbouring box he noticed a tribal leader sporting a traditional headdress. A veiled woman was seated behind him. The man spoke curtly to her and cussed. Everybody waited for the lights to go out. Meanwhile Salim watched the men and mostly young boys who filled all the second-class seats in the front section of the main floor.

They spit out watermelon seeds, bought soft drinks and soda water, and shouted at the top of their lungs. Farida sought the corner of the box where no one would see her. No need really, as who could identify this black shadow?

"I told them that I had to go to the dentist," she said and, as a further safeguard, spoke using one of the Muslim dialects.

"Do you have a toothache?"

"A little. Tomorrow I'll go to the dentist."

Salim felt both guilty and fortunate that a woman would endure a toothache and risk her reputation for him.

The lights finally went out but Salim didn't immediately sit next to Farida. He had waited his whole life for this moment but now that he at last had her to himself he hesitated and dared not make a move. What did he fear? By the sound of it, his neighbour had no such scruples. On the contrary, he behaved like an uncouth Bedouin.

"Salim," Farida said.

He moved his chair near hers. The two of them were finally together and by themselves. Farida lifted the veil from her face. She looked more beautiful than even in his wildest dreams. He loved her and would for the rest of his life. She offered Salim her hand which he eagerly took and caressed. He then lowered his head to kiss her palm and nibble her fingers. He would never let go of this hand. She took his and placed it on her lips. Meantime on the movie screen a father forced his daughter to marry a rich geezer. She cried and wailed as her mother tried to reason with her.

Their faces drew close and Farida kissed him like a child. Her lips tasted like fruit, a mix of grapes and watermelon.

"I will kiss you forever, until the end of my life," he vowed.

"Me too," she whispered and, emboldened, her tongue blazed a trail in his mouth. Her whole body sought his so as to give herself completely to him.

The movie screen voyeuristically espied these intimacies but their neighbours couldn't see them unless they leaned over their balconies. However, the boxes on the opposite side of the theatre faced Salim and Farida. He told himself that the people in them kept their eyes glued to the screen. He sat slightly higher in the seat, turned his back to the screen, and hugged her in order to shield Farida from prying eyes. He held her tight for himself, forever. He nervously covered one of her breasts with the palm of his hand. This startled her and she withdrew. But he then felt her hand inching up his thigh – only to stop suddenly. Their lips no longer parted except to catch their breath. They now breathed as one. Salim had lost all fear. He wanted the world to witness the celebration of his eternal marriage with Farida, to see that they shared the breath of life. She trembled more and more while her body jolted again and again. To muffle the sound of their passionate gasps, they locked jaws. When the lights turned back on, they jumped out of their seats.

Farida immediately veiled herself but Salim couldn't hide the wet spot on his pants. They sat silently without even looking at each other. The audience seemed to mock and condemn them. Oh what sweet nothings he would whisper in Farida's ear if they were alone. She offered him a handkerchief which, red-faced, he accepted. He would keep it for life. When they turned off the lights, he could discreetly wipe away the spot.

Darkness soon returned inside the theatre and Farida took the handkerchief from Salim to wipe his pants. All of a sudden she stopped, and fondled his penis.

She laughed with delight while he, overcome by happiness, couldn't find the words to express his love.

"I love you, Farida."

"Say it again."

"I love you, Farida."

She then sat up straight in her seat and with her hand on him said: "Now let's watch the film."

He could tell she said this tongue in cheek as a light-hearted way to convey her happiness and love.

AL BILDAD PLASTERED ON its front page:

Manhunt for Salim Abdullah

The next day *Al Zaman* announced:

Salim Abdullah turned himself in to the police

That same day *Al Istaklal*'s headline read:

Salim Abdullah Arrested

It went on to tersely report the arrest without giving any details. When caught in the act, the murderer had sworn that Salim Abdullah had paid him the precise sum of 25 dinars to kill Sasson Karkoukli. Why did Salim Abdullah want his brother-in-law dead? The hit man didn't know. The newspapers paid little attention to this Jewish incident which marginally involved Muslims. The tabloids would quickly relegate this story to their miscellaneous columns. After all, it didn't mark the first time that somebody murdered a man who had supposedly no enemies.

Al Bildad's third page briefly reported that Salim Abdullah vigorously maintained his innocence. The Jewish community breathed a sigh of relief that one of its members no longer made front page news and that the murder had become a peripheral matter. In cafés people went over and over the circumstances and motives surrounding the murder. Speculation ran wild. A third man, a Jew with close ties to Hakham Bashi, had apparently contracted with a Muslim to manage the slaughterhouses. Yet how would Sasson's murder help their business? Others argued that Ismaïl Hassan had acted on his own and had concocted this story to save his own skin. But did he have the brains to come up with such a scheme?

Another rumour was that Sasson's brother, Abraham Karkoukli, had plotted the whole thing to get back at Sasson and to gain sole control of the slaughterhouse contract. According to this story, as soon as this cheap, small time, country accountant moved to the city, he co-opted the wealth of these two inseparable friends. After all, why would Salim want his best friend, business partner, and brother-in-law to die? Those who claimed to be in the know whispered that this entire affair revolved around a mysterious woman whose identity they knew but dared not reveal. Some gave different explanations that entailed shady deals and often alluded to Abraham Karkoukli's jealousy, envy, and especially his greed. To think that this happened among Jews. They had resorted to the sordid practices of Bedouins.

Was it a coincidence or a secondary benefit? In any case the Jewish community stopped talking about the threats it faced. Everyone reverted to their old habits. Muslim, Christian, and Armenian children again beat Jewish children who ventured alone into side streets. Meanwhile, thanks to their good-naturedness, if not complicity, Jews returned to a daily fare of taunts and insults from others. At least the word Jew no longer amounted to a battle cry.

Salim Abdullah insisted on his innocence but the major newspapers now consigned this to the last page and didn't even use the adjective Jew before his name.

Young military officers who embraced Nazism spouted it in the newspapers. The Berlin government invited a former minister who trumpeted his admiration for the new regime and boasted that he had shaken the Fuehrer's hand. No mention of Jews since that could upset allies and raise animosity. Best to stay quiet on this subject. Anyway, didn't they have a common enemy, namely the British overlord, occupier and colonizer? Jews and Muslims alike readily acknowledged this in their shared struggle for independence.

A few weeks later newspapers dropped the Salim-Sasson story altogether and the Jewish community hardly spoke anymore about it. Not so, however, for the families directly affected by it.

Salim's mother had no chance to take sides. Due to her pregnancy, the Karkoukli family wouldn't let Najiah out of their house. Indeed they kept her sequestered in a room to protect her, and the deceased's posterity. By virtue of Najiah's pregnancy, she no longer belonged to the Abdullah family, or to herself. She had neither choice nor the strength to contest this. Abraham kept her under his thumb. She blindly obeyed him like a servant or a sheepish little girl.

She didn't really care what happened to her brother. Had Salim killed her husband as those around her claimed? She didn't even give it a moment's thought. As a widow carrying a fatherless child, that child's family – the Karkouklis – was now her family. Who else could she turn to in this tragedy? To her father who would do nothing more than say a prayer or recite the Psalms? To her brother who remained a student? To her mother who had indecorously hastened to marry her off?

In Abraham Karkoukli's eyes, Najiah, the widow and mother of a fatherless child, constituted living proof of Salim's guilt.

Meantime Salim's father, Selman Abdullah, retreated further and further into pietism. He rose at dawn and, before even putting on his phylacteries, he recited the Selichot. During the morning prayer the whole house heard him chanting the Psalms, if not reciting prayers and praises. Friends and neighbours honoured his wife Khatoun by addressing her as Oum Naji. But she was also Najiah and Salim's mother. Salim had become rich and orchestrated his sister's excellent marriage so that he had stopped playing second fiddle to his older brother Naji. On the contrary, Salim now represented the Abdullahs' pride and joy. More to the point, he earned the family's bread and butter. Indeed he had showered them all with gifts and money, besides renting them a house in Battawiyeen, a new neighbourhood.

Little wonder Naji no longer looked down on Salim. At first, Naji hadn't believed it, the fact his brother had made it big. Then he had become jealous and envious of Salim. But in the end Naji had recognized his brother's selfless generosity and ended up naively admiring him. In fact, Naji constantly vaunted Salim's merits and allowed none to question his goodness or his ability to accomplish anything he wanted.

When this catastrophe struck, their distraught family had only one recourse, namely that Salim, the accused himself, the miracle worker, would surely explain everything and make it alright. However, his mother had never seen him so fragile and helpless.

"Is it true?" she yelled at him, as though he were a little boy.
"No, I didn't kill him. I'm not a murderer."
"Are you innocent?" Naji dared ask.
"What do you mean?" Salim responded.

"Did you pay Ismaïl Hassan?"

"Don't tell me you believe that low-down, good for nothing crook?"

In the middle of the night Salim had gone to his office to gather up money and documents which he took with him to Karradah. He waited until dawn before going to Farida's house at Sulaykh. While he was away, a policeman delivered a summons to present himself as a witness at the police station.

"I'll come back for lunch," he had told his mother.

Who could she talk to? From whom could she seek advice? Should she go to Najiah and the Karkouklis? After all, Najiah was her daughter and Sasson was her son-in-law. She veiled herself and walked to Bab el Charqui. Abraham's wife opened the door and immediately shut it in her face.

"How dare you come here?" she shouted. "Go to your murderous son."

At noon, a policeman brought Salim back to his house.

"They're arresting me," he said in a raw voice.

He hastily stuffed shirts, sheets, and underwear in a sack. His father mumbled Psalms and his mother cried. Salim drew Naji into a corner of the room and slipped an envelope into his hand without the policeman seeing. Neighbours who had observed the family's meteoric rise stood silently in a circle around the door, now witnessing the Abdullahs' fall and humiliation. With the sack over his shoulder, Salim walked out trying to put on a self-assured smile. But his forlorn look belied it.

When Naji arrived at the specified address in Sulaykh, he thought he would be dealing with a lawyer. Fields surrounded the house which overlooked the river and the scent of jasmine and orange trees wafted from the garden. A servant in caretaker's clothes came to open the door. Naji handed him the letter yet the man remained as stiff as a board. He couldn't read so he awaited instructions.

"I want to see the man of the house," Naji said. This request made no sense to the caretaker who grew increasingly wary.

"Salim sent me."

The caretaker's face lit up.

"I'm his brother," Naji said.

"I'll inform Mme. Farida."

They walked together along a path lined with palm trees. Through their shadows Naji felt the autumn sun's warmth.

"Wait here," the caretaker said at the door into the house. Wicker chairs, tables, and lamps sat on the lawn.

A woman wearing a veil that did not cover her face stood at the doorstep.

"Naji!" she exclaimed.

"Agha," he stammered.

"I'm Farida, Farida Agha."

So he hadn't come to deal with a lawyer, but a songstress.

Photographs didn't do her justice. This young woman held centre stage in the limelight. Bewildered, Naji handed her the letter.

Farida, who stood barefoot, moved a few steps back. She seemed to take forever to decipher it.

"Will you see him today?" she asked.

"There are no visits permitted today. I'll go tomorrow, Thursday."

"Tell him not to worry. I'll do what he requests. I'll visit him."

Her face suddenly glowed.

"You look so much like Salim."

Early next morning Naji and his mother rode to the prison in a horse-drawn carriage. They wouldn't travel by bus lest they publicly display their shame.

No one could fail to notice Khatoun who veiled herself from head to toe. Most of the women there wore the blue, cotton veils of poor country folk. Khatoun's black, satin veil set her apart as a woman of means, to say nothing of Naji whose pants betrayed their social class, if not their ethnic origin. The noisy crowd comprised mainly women, a few children, as well as here and there a man who wore a *yashmagh*. People laughed and yelled while waiting for the prison to open. Khatoun had lost her fear. Sensing Naji's anxiety and unease, she said to herself that she didn't need him. With his pants and Jewish profile, he stuck out like a sore thumb. The next time she'd come alone and wear an old veil.

The door opened and the crowd surged into a long alley. Lined up behind bars, the prisoners called out and gestured with their hands as policemen brandished bayonets, shouted orders, and laughed.

Khatoun was having trouble trying to find Salim amidst the hordes of men who all looked the same. But then she

FARIDA

heard: "Naji, Naji." And Salim emerged, having blended perfectly with the mob. "He's so dark. His hair's so black," she thought. He seemed the spitting image of a Muslim. With a package tucked under her arm, she ploughed her way through the throng.

"Salim, what a disaster!" she wailed when she came face to face with him. "Oh my son, what's happened to us?"

She handed him the package with date squares, cheese bread and oranges. Naji drew near and held onto the bars.

"Did you give her my letter?" Salim asked.

"Yes. She says not to worry. She'll come to see you."

"When?"

"She didn't say."

"Was she alone?"

"The caretaker was there too."

"Did you go inside the house?"

"I stayed on the doorstep."

"And how was she?"

"Fine."

Embarrassment kept Naji from admitting that he had found Farida beautiful but that being over-emotional had reduced him to silence.

"So she told you that she would come?"

"Yes."

"Can you get any sleep here?" his mother asked. "Can you eat surrounded by these …"

Salim knew that underneath her veil tears trickled down his mother's cheeks. He felt alone, forsaken and despondent.

"It'll all work out," he said in a loud yet unsure voice.

He couldn't convince himself of it because his mother made him feel his wretchedness.

"How's my father doing?"

"He prays," Khatoun said with a mixture of pity and anger. "Naji will write his final exams in a month so that he can support himself. He'll teach in the government schools."

Unlike previously, this prospect no longer seemed pathetic to Salim. Naji had a life of freedom ahead of him whereas Salim had ... Farida. She'd watch his back and take care of everything. The two of them ...

He wanted to inquire about Najiah but didn't dare broach the subject. They would never again see that poor girl. Abraham wouldn't ever let her out of his clutches. He'd do anything to destroy Salim. He always had it out for him as Sasson's associate. It didn't help that Sasson had treated Abraham like an underling even though he was his older brother.

"Bring cigarettes the next time," he told Naji.

"Smoke to your heart's content, my son," Khatoun said. "It'll do you good."

"They're for gifts," he responded.

He couldn't wait for them to leave. They didn't help him in the least. On the contrary, they needed him and their dependence on Salim constituted a living reminder of his misfortune. He had fallen from the highest heights to the lowest depths. He now had to survive among these riffraff and buy the policemen's favours. Above all he needed right away to make sure that they did not take him for a rich Jew. Otherwise, they'd constantly put the squeeze on him. He would give them cigarettes as a gift and leave it at that.

When he had struck it big, his mother had started to pamper Salim, giving him the best portions at meals. But since his fall, she once again favoured Naji. Let them go to hell. They never loved him. Maybe Najiah ... but she would never have dared show him love. He'd fallen so low. He sat up straight and decided he wouldn't pity himself. He had no doubt that he'd get out of this fix.

SOMETIME BEFORE, ON A Saturday morning, a man had buttonholed Selman Abdullah at the synagogue exit.

"Father Naji."

Although he glanced at the man, Selman Abdullah did not reply. He went on murmuring a Psalm.

"Father Naji. I'm Abraham Karkoukli."

Selman's face remained expressionless.

"My brother Sasson is a friend of your son Salim."

"Oh yes! He's a good boy. May God protect him."

"In fact I want to talk to you about him."

It was autumn and the heat had abated. The two men walked slowly. Due to the fact it was the Sabbath, Abraham couldn't suggest that they go to a café, particularly since Selman lived two houses from the synagogue.

"Sasson's a wonderful boy. I'm not saying that because he's my brother. Salim will vouch for him. He doesn't drink. He doesn't gamble. He comes home every night and minds his own business."

Selman stood in front of his door waiting for Abraham to get to the point. It didn't cross his mind to invite him in.

"He's alone and that's not good. At his age I'd already been married a few years."

"May God help him."

"He has come several times to your home," Abraham stammered with visible embarrassment. "Your daughter, Najiah – may God protect her, served him an orangeade. She's the household's pride and joy, yet God wants daughters sooner or later to leave their parents. It's the law and there are no exceptions so we simply have to obey it. I know your daughter's young – may God grant her long life. However, she's reached the age when she can leave her mother and father. I'm only speaking for myself, as a brother who knows his brother's personality and wants the best for him. To some extent I'm also speaking as Salim's friend. I now work with these two business partners who're closer than brothers. I'm sure Sasson can make your daughter Najiah the happiest woman in the world. He can give her what her heart desires, especially a lifetime with an honourable man."

Selman understood and his face glowed. But he wondered what this had to do with him.

"You're Najiah's father and a man whom everyone respects. Young and old alike take their hats off to you."

"I must speak with Mother Naji."

"Of course. If it's OK with you, my wife will give her a visit."

A week went by before Abraham's wife, Chahla, knocked at the door. Khatoun nonchalantly received her. Najiah served an orangeade to Chahla who looked her up and down, her legs, arms, neck, and the way she walked. She had no apparent defects or deformities.

When all alone each of the two women waited for the other to begin speaking. Clothed in a red, ill-fitting dress that clearly delineated her fat folds, Chahla wore no make-up and put her black hair in a bun. She finally started the conversation by talking about the heat, the breeze and menfolk who work around the clock.

"My husband Abraham loves going to the office," she said, "but he's lazy compared to his brother Sasson. He tells me: 'Why would Sasson want to stay home?' He's right. Sasson has neither wife nor children. Abraham says Sasson needs to marry and once he does he'll become a new man because he'll work only for the well-being and happiness of his family."

"May God protect him. He and Salim are closer than brothers."

Najiah returned with coffee.

"I'm really putting you to a lot of trouble," Chahla said. "May God grant that we next meet at Najiah's wedding."

Najiah didn't react at all. Instead she immediately left the two women.

"She's truly the lady of the house," Chahla said. "May God protect her."

"In reality she's just a child, though many want to marry Najiah. Her father responds that she's not yet old enough for marriage."

"Nonetheless, children grow up. Then the right time comes and you must not pass it up. One day we see a young girl and close our eyes. When we open them, she's already a mature woman. Time flies but she's the same person. Mother Naji, you know why I'm here. Sasson should not stay single. You know him."

"He's like my son. May God protect him."

Both women knew that they had virtually sealed the deal. They simply needed to iron out the details: date, ceremony, dowry, terms, etc. Sasson had duly advised Chahla that he wouldn't insist on a dowry, money, or furniture. He would pay for the ceremony and accept the dress she wore as the entirety of her trousseau.

The next week they got engaged and set the wedding day for the beginning of winter, after Sukkot.

Salim wondered how Sasson would now deal with certain issues. No longer was he merely a friend, a business partner, much less a stranger. From hereon he belonged to the same family whose honour and interests he must uphold. They were thus all in the same boat.

At the office Sasson tried hard to play it cool but talked too artificially about letters to write, companies, and the immediate future. Salim saw through Sasson's relaxed veneer, saw that he sought to hide something. A new intimacy arose between them but they did not know what form it would take, or how to handle it. As a result, it represented a threat, like that of the unknown.

"I won't go anymore to the house at Karradah," Sasson said as they left the office.

Salim felt relieved and happy. He wanted to hug Sasson in appreciation for acting in a way that Salim didn't even dare dream he would. Instead he settled for giving him a smile.

"You can have the house for the time being," Sasson said. "I'll pay my half of the rent for a while. Then you can make up your mind."

How could he share his joy with Sasson? How could he tell him that he too would soon celebrate his wedding, in love and happiness, albeit secretly and far from prying eyes? How could he reveal that a woman loved him so much that she put her reputation and life on the line for him? He ached to shout from the rooftops that Farida was the most beautiful of women, the greatest singer, and a lover without equal.

Sasson couldn't match this. Najiah was another matter. Love? Perhaps. A love that little by little would develop naturally through day-to-day living rather than through words. A love that would unfold within the confines of mundane existence and without risks. Lovemaking. Najiah was his sister and Salim couldn't imagine her hand on a man's thigh and French kissing him.

He would have the house to himself. No Nadia. No Nouriah. It would host their secret honeymoon and serve as the home of love. Once word of this got out, he would confront his mother and sister – indeed the whole world. Farida would become his wife; in fact, she already was. His family? Mothers and fathers don't matter; only a man and a woman in love count, especially when the two decide to live as one. Night and day would meld into each other for Salim and Farida. Someday he would reveal his happiness and good fortune to Sasson; however, that day had not yet come.

THE DAY BEFORE THEIR meeting Salim went to the house in Karradah. A cleaning lady worked there once a week. The icebox had no ice but autumn had subdued the heat. He changed the sheets, put a vase of flowers on the table and tried not to think about Farida. Like a despondent caged animal, he nervously paced back and forth.

One of Nouriah's hairpins lay near the bed yet she remained far from his thoughts. He pictured her alone in the empty house and sensed a twinge of nostalgia mixed with affection. But he didn't in the least desire her. Farida loomed larger than life, albeit in a place accessible only to Salim. There, his body and he would give way to the words they uttered while gazing at each other.

They had the whole afternoon because she once again claimed that she needed to see the dentist whose always overcrowded waiting room operated on a first come, first serve basis.

During their last date at El Saadoun Park, he mentioned that, because of Sasson's engagement, the house had become Salim's and that he and Farida could have it to themselves. Her immediate acceptance surprised him. She didn't fear the consequences. Had she no concern for her honour? He rented a carriage not far from his office and picked up Farida at Bab el Charqui near the clock tower. Her silence and the long ride enabled him to calm down.

Farida removed her veil. She wore a cotton dress with a large flowery pattern. She appeared dainty and fragile to him. Did she realize the risk she ran? He wouldn't forsake her. He'd protect her and devote his life to their love. She leaned over to breathe in the flower's scent. He brought her a glass of water. Quiet and docile, she seemed an abandoned little girl who was at his mercy. Standing side by side, they felt self-conscious about their bodies and dared not look at each other.

To celebrate Farida's visit, Salim had dreamt of inviting the whole town to a dinner party with an orchestra.

"Does your tooth still hurt?" he asked.

She put her face close to his and opened her mouth.

"See, it's this one."

In order for him to touch the tooth, she took his hand and that set him on fire. He led her into the bedroom, having already drawn the drapes. Their naked bodies met and melded. With fearless determination, Farida looked straight into Salim's eyes. For a split second, he told himself that he was about to ruin the reputation and life of the woman he loved. However, he dismissed this thought by telling himself that he loved her and always would so that no harm could befall her. She was even faster than him, as though she wanted to cross the Rubicon once and for all. In the face of the mortal sin, she chose the perilous path of the unknown.

She let out a long, shrill, painful cry, then tightly hugged him and began to hiccup. Only when their bodies separated did Salim realize that he had blood all over him. He leaned on his elbow to gaze at Farida. She had contentment, gratitude and

FARIDA

serenity written on her face. He held her life and reputation in his hands. He would never desert her. Desire overwhelmed him so he hugged her even more tightly to chase away the fears and dangers that lurked about.

They lingered in the bed waiting, it seemed, for the clock to strike the moment of their birth as a couple. The world would thus know that these youngsters had found their place in the sun. Now that they had suddenly become adults, the two of them decided to drink life to the lees.

"I love you," Salim kept saying. In one flash, he worshipped her, worried about the future, and couldn't wait for tomorrow. With a resolute, determined look Farida whispered simply: "I love you too."

He daydreamed about their lives together and envisioned himself nightly arriving home to the sounds of children, his children, while he brought in a bag of groceries and Farida awaited him amidst her daily tasks. Other times he imagined her on the roof of a house he bought her in Battawiyeen or Ulwiyah. There she sang her heart out so that he could not tear himself away from home and no longer wanted to go to the office. They would keep to themselves. Neither his family nor hers existed, or at best they would remain in the background.

Those who witnessed Farida and Salim's all-conquering love would stand in awe and applaud them. Of all the women in the world Farida alone dared proclaim her love, dared risk her reputation and life, for a man. Truth be told, Salim didn't know any movie star as beautiful as Farida, or any singer whose voice matched hers, and no woman moved as gracefully as her, even when she lay her head on a pillow.

Salim wanted to speak about all this with Sasson but Sasson had his hands full with his imminent wedding and had a one-track mind: Buy, buy, buy. How could you blame him? As for Najiah, she lived in a soulless, bygone era.

Salim had to wait three days before Farida could return again to Karradah. Without saying a word, their bodies fused as soon as they walked through the door. No blood this time; their sweat alone mingled.

"You're cautious," she cried.

Her eyes betrayed no fear. They looked indomitable and sparkled with love.

"You're my wife. We're the first and only couple to celebrate the true wedding of two lives that seals forever their indestructible love."

She turned gloomy.

"Don't you believe me?" he asked.

"Yes, my love, I believe you. I'm your wife and always will be, no matter what happens. I'll never love anyone else."

"So let's get married, I mean for real, not just here …"

She gazed into the distance as if longing for bygone days or lost heirlooms.

"I'll inform my family of my decision," he said, "and go see your biological parents at Hilla. I want to meet them and thank them for bringing you into the world."

Farida burst out laughing.

"Salim, you always know the right words to make me happy."

"They're not mere words …"

He again sensed her getting distant.

"Don't you believe me?" he asked again.

"Yes. Come what may, I will always trust you. No matter what you do, I'll never lose faith in you."

He didn't understand why she spoke in riddles and virtually wished him goodbye.

"Let's set a date for our marriage," he said. "How about in two months so that we have time to find a house and furnish it?"

He then whispered in her ear: "I won't need anymore to take precautions. You'll bear me a son, and then a daughter who will sing and dance as well as you."

The sombre, almost frozen expression on her face alarmed him.

"I'm a singer, Salim."

"I'll listen to you day and night, from dawn to dusk, as my daily bread."

"I want to sing in public, Salim."

This took him aback and made no sense to him.

"But where? Not in a nightclub!"

"We're in Baghdad and here there's no other place than a nightclub."

"But, Farida, nightclub singers ..."

"I know. They're prostitutes."

"Why Farida? We're getting married. It's not because of ..."

He stared at the bed.

"Salim, you're my only pride and joy. I'll let no other man into my life."

"Farida, we're getting married."

"I must sing or I'll die. Your wife's a singer and she'll shout her love from the roof tops."

"Farida, we're not in a movie and Baghdad isn't America. Don't you realize what type of people hang out at nightclubs? There's no singer who can ..."

"I answer to you and you alone for my reputation. I know you never can nor will leave me because you love me. You told me that I'm the greatest singer in the world and I believe you. Just wait and see, Salim."

"But not in nightclubs with men who … You're my wife, Farida."

"I'm your wife and, as long as I'll sing of my love for you and with you there by my side, together we'll celebrate our love, so that each day we'll renew our marriage."

She stepped away from him. He had no choice but to follow her or she would disappear into the unknown and he would never see her again.

SASSON'S WEDDING TOOK PLACE in his new home. Abou Nouas Street led to it along the river's edge. A gentle slope served as the path for a future street. Built European-style and surrounded by vacant land, the house seemed to rise straight out of the sand. Rather than adjoining a courtyard, all the rooms stood in a row to form the house. A staircase offered access to the roof. Since it was autumn, it proved too brisk to hold the wedding on the roof. Sasson paid for everything. Najiah came out the winner in this wedding because the dress on her back constituted the entirety of both her trousseau and dowry. The Abdullah family, namely Khatoun, insisted on a discreet ceremony with few guests, a chamber orchestra, and at midnight a vocalist to end the evening. Sasson bustled about overseeing it all while Salim austerely received the guests. Ladies, especially those who had marriageable daughters, told him: "Now it's your turn."

He perfunctorily gave each of them the same, curt answer: "I must wait for my older brother Naji to get married."

Those very same women badgered Khatoun to get started looking for wives for Naji and Salim.

The world has changed, she responded. What say does a mother have? Sons nowadays do as they please.

She didn't dare mention that Naji still needed to complete his studies and that she knew nothing about Salim's life.

The wedding singer possessed a limited vocal range. They had to keep quiet to hear her. Salim initially relished the fact that she couldn't hold a candle to Farida but subsequently pitied those compelled to applaud her. He then physically felt Farida's absence. It was she and their wedding that they should be celebrating. Yet how could he resent those poor mothers who naively offered their daughters to him? How could he announce that he wasn't an eligible bachelor? That he had married the most beautiful woman in the world? He could picture the smirks on their faces: a singer ... someone to cavort with before marrying a respectable family's daughter.

A week later Sasson first mentioned the contract for exclusive rights to kosher slaughter. His brother Abraham would partner with them and they could count on the Al Shaikhli family which included a lawyer who had won a case for them in the courts.

"We know nothing about meat and slaughtering," Salim argued.

"What did we know about fabrics, wheat, household appliances, and leather before we imported them?"

"It's not the same thing," Salim said in protest.

"What's the difference? We buy, we sell, we make a profit. But in this case we'll have no competitors; we'll have a monopoly."

To tell the truth, Salim agreed with the idea. They normally hashed out business matters by one of them making a proposition and the other critiquing it. Once convinced, they went full speed ahead.

"You'll go by yourself to the slaughterhouses," Salim said. "I can't stand the stench of meat."

They broke into laughter.

FARIDA

"I have to leave that family," Farida declared the moment they were alone in Karradah. Since she had her own keys, she came in the afternoon whenever she could get away. However, she had started running out of reasons to absent herself. The string of excuses stretched from the dentist, to a brother who refused to darken the doorstep of his aunt and uncle's house, to errands at the fruit market, and even to catching a movie in the morning!

Farida's aunt couldn't keep her in check and feared that she would leave for good to God knows where. By raising his voice at Farida, her uncle thought he'd done his job. She terrified him. At any moment she could "fall," that is to say, become a prostitute. If he were a Bedouin, he would lock her up in her room and, if that failed, he would publicly slit her throat to preserve the family's honour.

He was not her father, or his brother, but only the husband of her aunt. To be brief, he was an outsider.

"I can't stand them anymore," Farida said. "I'm a maid, a slave who receives only bread and water."

Salim understood the family. He visualized himself as an unscrupulous Muslim pimp who would exploit Farida, then use her in a whorehouse. She had lost her honour and all hope of marriage. However, Salim loved her and this love restored her honour and lifted her out of the degradation into which she had recently sunk as a fallen woman. He was an honourable man and would defend her come what may.

"I told them that I want to learn music," she said as they put their clothes back on at nightfall.

Salim remained silent in the face of this declaration. Farida didn't simply dream of becoming a singer in the future.

"I thought of Sami, the blind violinist," she went on to say. "I told him that I'd go to his house. But why not have him come here? You could even attend the lessons. His brother will bring him and you can take them back."

"But you don't want to become a violinist, do you?"

"Sami can play anything. I want to learn the oud in order to accompany myself and to compose my own songs."

"You want, you want to …"

"Salim, you're not opposed to me, are you? You're my man, my love. You're my husband ten times over. Nothing can separate us. My whole life I'll sing only for you. Even where there's a crowd, I'll sing just for you. I'll spend my life saying I love you. Salim, you can't be my enemy. Tomorrow, you'll go see Sami."

He didn't answer.

"Do you promise?" she said half gently half irritably. "Do you promise?" she repeated with a hint of intimidation.

"I'll try."

"Promise me you'll go."

His head nodded in agreement.

When he arrived at the office, to his surprise Sasson was there.

"I was waiting for you, Salim."

"Oh!"

"You need to explain your absences. You're never here in the afternoon. Do you run another business?"

"What are you driving at?"

"I don't want to tail you, Salim, but you're gone every afternoon."

"I go to Karradah."

"To the house?"

He seemed relieved.

"If only you would have let me know. So you're servicing both of them. That's too much for one man. Does Nadia treat you nice?"

Salim thought he sensed disapproval and restrained anger in Sasson's voice.

"I've not seen Nadia nor Nouriah again. That's over, Sasson."

"Did you get married without telling me?" He roared with laughter.

"Yes, I'm married, Sasson. Someday you'll meet my wife. I need you to wait until then. Can you wait?"

Beside himself with exasperation, he begged Sasson to understand and not to ask questions. He just had to remain patient. They left the office together.

"Come see your sister," Sasson said.

"Not this evening. I want to walk."

They went along Al Rachid Street, stopped a while in front of the Mashaal store that showcased Oldsmobile's latest model, then continued to the Al Zawraa movie house which featured Robert Taylor and Loretta Young. A little farther along they saw a new Chevrolet on display at the Lawee store.

"I want to buy a car," Sasson said. "But Najiah's afraid. She says she had a dream and a premonition that ... You must talk to her. She'll listen to you."

When they arrived at the door, Salim stood still and didn't seem ready to leave.

"Come in. It'll make Najiah happy to see you."

"No, not tonight."

The tone of Salim's voice then changed.

"I too have a wife," he said both defiantly and despairingly. "I love a woman, Sasson, and she loves me. She sacrificed her life for me ..."

"Is she Christian? Muslim?"

"No, Jewish like you and me."

"She's from a family that ..."

"A respectable family."

"Do you want me to speak to her father?"

"No. It's not that ... How do I explain this ... We love each other, Sasson. It's a lifelong love."

"That's no problem."

"We're married, but not in the eyes of others."

"Do you mean ...?"

"Yes, you got it."

"Are you ashamed of her? Or her family?"

"Of course not. I love her."

"I know you love her. That's fine in the movies."

"She loves me too, Sasson. She's given her life for me."

Salim suddenly did a one-eighty and ran down the slope. He stood a long time facing the river, in the shadows, tears running down his cheeks.

LATE THE NEXT MORNING he went to the place where Sami gave violin lessons in the midst of the covered street market, above a grocer's shop. Daylight could hardly penetrate into the room which had a table, two chairs, two stools, and a bench, along with a pitcher topped by a glass. Sami sat in a corner wearing sunglasses and, it seemed, a smile. He dictated Western musical notes to a ten-year-old boy who played in front of him. To illustrate his instructions Sami suddenly grabbed the violin. Emotion overcame Salim as he felt the sound rise in pitch and permeate his skin. All at once Sami stopped, then gathered his sheet music, and put his violin in its case. Salim closed the door behind him.

"I've come about private lessons," he said. "They're not for me."

"Oh."

"Could you come to the house?"

"For your son?"

"No, my wife."

She wanted to learn to play the oud to accompany herself, he explained.

She was primarily a singer. "One of the best," he added.

Sami would come to the house with his younger brother who needn't wait there since Salim would accompany Sami home.

"I TOLD MY AUNT that I am taking music lessons," Farida said. "I warned her that, if she opposed me, I would leave home and sing in a nightclub for money to rent an apartment. She gave in because she had no choice. She's convinced that she can't keep me from 'falling' and losing my honour. She wants to hold on to me as long as possible since it's hard to find a maid who works for free. That woman has the attitude of some bitch running a brothel. She perceives all women as prostitutes and despises her husband who pays through the nose for the slightest favour from her."

They arrived one hour before Sami. Farida hugged Salim so tight that she almost crushed him. "You'll never leave me and I'll always be your woman." Her gratitude, like her demands, constituted a facet of her love. "Someday the whole world will say Farida's a great singer and I'll love you for being the first to tell me this. I'll make you proud of me and spend my life singing for you."

When he saw Sami place Farida's fingers on the oud's strings, Salim felt a pang of jealousy. A man touched Farida's hand, albeit a blind teacher, he kept saying to himself so as to calm down. He couldn't wait for this ordeal to end.

It seemed as though she already knew how to play and simply took up again an instrument she'd barely put down.

Sami repeated the notes which she instinctively knew. Farida started singing to herself, then, gazing at Salim, she sang to thank him and to express her love and happiness. His eyes caressed her and without touching they made love. Oscillating between tenderness and tempestuousness, her voice created an unbearable tension that overwhelmed them because nothing mitigated the momentous sensation of their bodies bursting. Salim felt engulfed and imbued. He would do anything for her, even rob or murder. Through song Farida told him that her life no longer belonged to herself. Instead she offered it to him body and soul through this eternal, consummate song.

"I have nothing to teach you," Sami said when she stopped.

"I can't read music," she responded with exuberance.

"You don't need to. The music's in you."

"I want to learn to play. How to begin and end."

"I'll teach you what you already know better than I."

The three of them left together in a carriage.

Sami didn't ask any questions. Why did your wife leave the house with us? Where are you going? He lived on El Torate Street near the Alliance Française school. Salim suggested dropping off Farida but she refused.

"I want to drive through the city with you," she said after leaving Sami at his front door. "I'm not afraid. I want to shout out my love so that everyone hears. Salim, I'm incredibly happy."

He was afraid. Despite winter's fast approach, from every rooftop jealous, hostile eyes looked down on them in judgement. No one could live love in this city. It had wives and prostitutes not women in love, much less loved. Only Farida and Salim went against the grain in this city where their pluck set them apart. Nonetheless, he was afraid.

SAMI AND HIS BROTHER went to Karradah two or three times a week. Salim arrived after them. He wondered if Sami came for the sheer pleasure of hearing Farida. He thought that he too …What if she decided never to sing again? He couldn't visit her anymore. He could no longer love her. Sami's brother sometimes stayed for the lessons in order to accompany him home. Farida improvised on the oud when all alone. With a forlorn, faraway look she gave voice to love's bliss and sorrow, to the expectation and absence of love. Her eyes alternately beckoned and bestowed.

At such moments Salim wanted nothing more than to hold her tight so that their naked bodies found shelter from the world and its perils. He wanted to protect her and witness her development in the weeks and months to come. The Karradah hideaway enabled him to take care of her yet keep their secret while she continued to sing and proclaim her love.

One evening Farida told him in a firm voice: "Sami's brother went home with him. I've decided to spend the night here and don't want you to leave me so you're going to stay here, too. Sami's brother will advise your mom that you're overnighting at a party. She won't worry."

"Did you advise your family?"

"Yes. It's they who obey me. They know that I can leave and that they have no way to stop me. They're scared. My aunt's already given up. She thinks I'm now 'fallen.' A whore. She just hopes that the word doesn't get around. Her husband privately gloats over the idea of a prostitute on his wife's side of the family because that puts her at his mercy. They don't have a daughter to marry off but it may prove difficult, though not impossible, for their son."

Then she continued: "I spoke to Sami. I asked for his advice. I want to sing. I mean to sing in public."

Salim felt himself falling to pieces.

"Where? Not in a nightclub?"

"Where else? I'm not in Cairo to sing in films. I'm not Umm Kulthum who calls the shots."

"But, Farida, you know who hangs out in nightclubs."

"I know. Men who drink, listen to music, and who ..."

She stopped there. Salim knew that she had finished the sentence in her head but that the words would not come out.

"Sami's part of the orchestra at the Al Zawraa nightclub."

And to think that Salim had sought out this man and brought him into his home.

"He'll speak to the owner. Anton, an Armenian."

"Farida," Salim shouted, "you know what they expect of nightclub women. You know what kind of life dancers and singers lead."

"I know, Salim."

Now on the verge of tears, she seemed to call for help from the bottom of an abyss.

"You can't, Farida."

She rose, then he heard her hiccupping in the kitchen. He loved an "artist." The woman to whom he gave his life decided she was going to sing in nightclubs. "I love an artist," he told himself. A prostitute's OK but who's your wife and where are your children? An artist's something altogether different, like a mistress or a whore. Only fools and idiots devote their lives to such women. They don't restrict themselves to love. They don't limit the numbers of men and lovers who look after them and pay for their upkeep.

Farida's crying deeply moved him. He couldn't leave her to fend for herself. Yet she had decided to leave him and plunge into sleazy bars where drunks hang out. It was she who had chosen to "lower herself" to a dissolute life of men and lovers who buy a woman's favour. She didn't even need to do that. He would give everything ... a house, a home ...

She came back in and over her flowery dress she slipped on a sweater which she herself had knit. "Someday," she said, "I'll knit you a sweater. Promise." She would also cook, bear children that they would raise ... She had regained her resolve, a resolve that came out in an unshakeable smile. She would soon start singing and that would mark the point of no return.

"Why, Farida?"

"I can't resist, Salim. It's stronger than me."

She said this with neither a hint of regret nor a second thought on the matter. Men could line up in front of her door and she would welcome them with that inscrutable smile which kept them at arm's length. She drew close and tenderly yet firmly looked at him.

"Salim, I love you and my life belongs to you. I'll never love or let another man into my life."

"So why then?"

"I can't help myself."

She spoke calmly but not coldly, as though he were a child and she was his mother or big sister.

He undressed and bedded her. She offered no resistance. On the contrary Farida anticipated his every move. She responded to a call and in turn called out. Salim didn't possess her any more than she possessed him. He wanted her and without reservation she freely, whole heartedly gave herself to him. They couldn't keep up with their bodies which hastened to one another. Seduction proved superfluous since they needed neither persuading nor convincing. The facts spoke for themselves. Together they sought, albeit each in their own way, to connect with the other and live out their love. He too had crossed the Rubicon. Tomorrow, he'd announce he would be leaving her. Because of his jealousy, he couldn't accept her seeing other men and he would show his rivals no mercy. He refused to share his life with a prostitute. Tomorrow, he'd tell her for sure, but today belonged to them.

This morning marked their birth and this evening would seal their love. Such precious gifts come all too rarely in life. He wanted to shield her from all attacks and to stave off any intruder. She suddenly began to sing. She sang new lyrics about the Tigris River, the man in her life and love. The melody echoed those of many songs yet he had never before heard it. She continually repeated, modulated, and improvised the melodic line like a circle in a spiral. Her vibrato gave him goose bumps all over his body. He loved her and there was no escaping it. Her voice and the exquisite tenderness she showed him held him captive. She sang for him, and him alone.

She said: "Salim you can't leave me. I sing for you. I can only sing for you."

"Why then Anton's nightclub with all its Muslim men who buy drinks and women? Why …?"

How could he challenge, much less oppose her when she loved him so much that it overwhelmed him? He wanted her all to himself and she wanted the whole world to witness her love for him. He couldn't bear the thought of Farida on stage at a nightclub where drunken, lecherous men's eyes ogled, undressed, and violated her while he idly stood by as a mere spectator in the audience. No, never in a million years would he allow those hordes of barbarous cannibals to dissect and eat her body.

"It's a new song," she said. "Sami brought me a journal he knows, *Al-Hassid*, whose poems and stories come from Jewish writers. I chose a poem and changed some of its words. The young man dreams about an imaginary love. He doesn't realize that a person can live out their love, that the man a woman loves can really exist, that his body has its own odour, and that his arms can hug the woman he loves."

Salim couldn't keep pace with her. He had to follow Farida and would soon have to run to catch up with her. Before he knew it, she wouldn't remember what he looked like. He felt powerless in her presence but he couldn't devote his life to an "artist," hide their relationship, or share her body with others. Yet the thought of not seeing her again made his knees buckle and his body go limp. He just wanted to disappear.

Once or twice a week they spent the night together. As soon as one fell asleep the other would wake him or her up. It seemed they feared that time would slip through their fingers and that life would pass them by.

"You'll be tired tomorrow," she said.

"It doesn't matter. I don't want to sleep."

At dawn one day, Salim felt Farida's hands, then her legs, and then her entire body on his. Although he pretended to doze, Farida touched and aroused him.

"I've decided to leave my aunt's home," she said a little later.

"To go where?"

"I first thought about renting a house, but I don't have the money. I can't stand it any more and I can't keep making up excuses every time I go out."

"You won't return to your home town, will you?" he said in a fit of panic.

"No, don't worry, I'm fine here."

"You could move into this house," he said hesitantly.

"At last!" she said, bursting out laughing. "I was waiting for you to offer it."

She lay on top of him.

"As soon as I start to earn money, I'll move to another house."

Relieved, yet worried, Salim stopped questioning Farida for fear that he would specifically have to condone and countenance her behaviour. She waited a week before telling him by bits and pieces about meeting Anton and her booking with him.

Located where the Akoulia and Senak neighbourhoods converge, the nightclub had a nondescript front door sandwiched between a jeweller's and a watchmaker's shops. Inside, the nightclub featured a large, raised room used in the winter. During the summer it operated outdoors onto a nearby street.

A small man, with slightly greying hair and a bulging belly, Anton wore a big smile that showed off all his gold teeth. His protruding eyes waited for Farida to remove her veil while Sami and his brother sat there in silence.

"Sami keeps vaunting your voice," Anton said, tentatively speaking in the Jewish dialect.

"He's an excellent teacher," she responded with a Muslim accent so as to cut short any attempt to butter her up.

"You won't sing veiled, will you?" Anton asked. His apparently casual, encouraging laugh masked his obvious unease.

She removed her veil, folded and laid it on a chair. Sami mounted the stage and began to improvise on the oud. He played an introduction and the first bars of some songs just as he would before an audience. He knew how to change registers in such a way that he announced the singer's arrival onstage, built up anticipation of their voice, accompanied, and highlighted it. Sami seemed so close yet so far from the singer because he took a back seat to their voice.

Farida stood alone in front of all the empty seats. She avoided Anton's gaze. He leered at her and, like the packs of lascivious men who would come there, he stripped her naked with his eyes. How could she evade those eyes that strove to trap and imprison her? Salim's hostile look didn't help. He disapproved of her conduct. She momentarily resented that he loved her but that, instead of standing by his woman, he had shunned her and let her unveil before a stranger, a man who would like a beast molest her with the full weight of his body if she didn't defend herself.

Sami changed registers, thus giving Farida her cue. Her compelling voice disguised her fear and insecurity. Yet she couldn't hide from Anton's eyes which mirrored those of countless men. She stood exposed, vulnerable, and within easy reach. Anton's gaze easily uncovered all her secrets. She shed her body so as to become pure, floating voice. Anton's inscrutable look enveloped her secret but left Farida herself untouched. Singing sealed her off from all attempts to encroach on her. Her voice erected an impregnable wall that no man could breach as she resolutely set her sights beyond the horizon. First Salim's eyes, then his face, then his whole body emerged from the shadows. He informed her every move and each inflection of her voice no matter how slight. She sang for him and him alone. Salim's presence kept her out of Anton's voracious grasp and made Farida inaccessible to him so that he could only applaud her.

"You're the greatest, most sublime singer in Iraq," Anton said. "Sami, have you ever heard such a divine voice? All the Syrian, Lebanese and Egyptian songstresses will bow down before you."

Farida knew that henceforth Anton would consider her untouchable and never suggest that they spend an evening much less the night together, for him to learn more about her singing. Her voice stood on its own merits.

"You'll start in two weeks which will give me enough time to put up a billboard above the entrance, place posters all along Rachid Street, buy full-page ads in the newspapers, and get publicity into cafés and offices. I'll plaster the city with your name and Al Zawraa will become the most famous nightclub in Iraq. Your fame will spread to Beirut, Damascus and Cairo."

Farida insisted on 50 dinars a month which amounted to six times her uncle's salary. She also secured a day off, and more importantly, the right not to sit at customers' tables.

"But you're not married …," Anton started to say.

"Yes. I am. My husband's wealthy and influential."

"Oh. Who is he?" Anton asked with a sceptical smile.

"You'll find out. He'll come with me."

The thought of having a diva who didn't mingle with his patrons appealed to Anton. Umm Kulthum never drank with country bumpkins and Leila Mourad did not sleep with soldiers. Now Baghdad would have its own singing sensation whose voice and powerful husband would shelter her.

How could Farida break the news to Salim? She waited until the moment right after they made love, while they lay naked and he still held her tightly in his arms.

"You're hugging the new star of Al Zawraa nightclub."

He let go of her and remained silent.

"Do you have nothing to say?"

"You didn't ask my opinion so what can I say?"

"I told you, dearest, that Sami would speak to Anton."

"Sami, Sami. That's all you ever talk about."

"Salim, my love, don't get mad. You'll be as proud of me as I am of you. The new star will sing to you alone. I can only sing for you."

"And a few hundred drunks and lowlifes."

"Salim, you are and always will be the only one for me. If you leave me, I'll kill myself."

"No threats, Farida."

She moved into the house at Karradah but Salim didn't visit and staying there alone at night frightened her. The winter wind made her even more afraid. She had told her aunt that she was going back to Hilla, her home town. Yet Farida knew that neither she nor her husband believed this. It wasn't their fault if Farida had "fallen." As long as she had lived with them, they had looked out for her honour and theirs. However, when the devil takes hold of a young girl, nobody can stop her – not a man or a woman, not an aunt or an uncle.

At the office Salim seemed faraway and lacklustre. He agreed to everything Sasson said and in this vein they decided to go into the slaughterhouse business.

Then came the rains. It poured cats and dogs. Little unpaved streets turned into swamps. To avoid the mud, people walked alongside walls and only ventured outside if necessary. Water dripped from leaky roofs into rooms while the poor bore the brunt of the driving rain. Everyone awaited a rainbow to signal that the storm had passed. Salim got upset with Farida and she with him. Didn't he know that she loved him and would give her life for him? She asked Sami to visit her everyday and to loan her money since she had none.

Five days went by without any news from Salim. She couldn't believe he had dumped her just like that. No man she loved would behave this way. She asked Sami's brother to go to Salim's office.

"Tell him that the bank's manager sent you."

He came back breathless and covered with mud. It proved rough going to get around the city. Although the rain had stopped, large puddles of water blanketed streets and made them slippery. At any moment you could fall flat on your back.

"Salim's sick," he reported.

"My heart knew it, and I can't go to his bedside."

"Don't worry, he's doing better. The fever's gone down though he still coughs. They had a doctor come who prescribed rest. Here, Salim sent you this."

He handed Farida money and she burst into tears.

"What message did he give you for me?"

"He couldn't talk because his mother always hovered over him."

"He thinks about me, doesn't he? Did he tell you if I can visit him? He needs me."

"He gave me the money for you and asks you to wait for him."

"Wait for him. Of course, I'll wait for him. How could I do otherwise?"

She didn't see him until the day before her first engagement at the nightclub. He arrived in the afternoon, walking slowly, as though he had difficulty finding his footing.

"You look very pale. Come lie on the bed."

She became motherly without any sexual overtones. To Salim she seemed like a girl who had grown into a woman, like his sister Najiah, or his mother. Like all women she appeared to care only for a man's well-being, which made her ordinary. Had he dreamt up Farida? Did she represent a figment of his imagination? He so seldom saw her. When she sang, he forgot everything including his body and hers. She had a small, fragile body with dark skin and hair. Indeed, he had never realized how much she looked like a Muslim through and through. While sick the image of her constantly came to mind and comforted Salim. Although too weak to feel sexual desire, he later envisioned her lying naked beside him and he couldn't wait for that moment. Now with her there he rediscovered a familiar albeit distant world of hidden goodness and bliss.

Farida trembled.

"If you only knew how much I love you. Come hear me sing. Please come."

She reminded him of a little girl who felt quite guilty and asked for acceptance rather than forgiveness.

"Why are you so cruel to me? If you don't come, I'll kill myself. I can't live without you."

Her plea left him cold. He pictured their lives unfolding like a movie in which he loves her, she sings, becomes a star and he loses her. He should have put his foot down, but it was too late now. Their chance had come and gone. Although he loved her, it was his turn to seek absolution. His love had faded by fits and starts into his memory and he couldn't reclaim it, much less make it live again. He'd go as a special guest and, at her insistence, he would not reveal their relationship so that nobody knew. For this she would absolve him. However, he would never again go to hear her. He couldn't publicly take pride in a singer. On the contrary, he pitied Farida and her absentee love. Perhaps someday she'd come back to him.

FARIDA WENT ALONE TO the nightclub. Salim had promised to sit in the audience.

The orchestra gave each of its musicians the opportunity to showcase his virtuosity by improvising on his instrument. They began with the oud, then the kanoun, the ney, and finally the violin, which Sami played.

Salim ordered a quart of arak. While waiting, he looked the audience up and down. "Not a Jew in sight," he said to himself. However, some of the soldiers, sheikhs and bureaucrats certainly fit the image of Muslims. Men often sat two at a table, if not three or four. They talked loudly and laughed raucously while guzzling arak. Salim didn't feel comfortable. He should have invited Sasson. But that meant having to give Najiah an explanation which she would then have recounted to her mother who would have told Naji the news. And Salim would never hear the end of it.

His face got hot and he worried about his fever returning. He drank quickly to calm his nerves because he found himself in foreign territory. Even though he crossed daily in front of this establishment, he didn't recognize anyone in it. Here he represented an intruder, an outsider.

Anton introduced Farida as the nightclub's great discovery and Al Zawraa's new star. She appeared in a long, black dress with a sequinned neckline and sleeves. She wore no makeup, yet a slight smile softened her stern demeanour. To Salim she seemed larger than life and so dominated the stage that the audience fell silent. She nodded her head to acknowledge their applause then waited for the orchestra to slow the rhythm in order for her to start singing an improvisation. *Ya laili ya aini.* In a low but solid voice, she at first sang simple modulations with a strong melody, followed by increasingly complex variations that took on a life of their own and rose to a crescendo that completely permeated the nightclub.

Although a member of the audience, and seated in its midst, Salim forgot everyone else as he hung on this woman's every word. He saw Farida in a new light and loved her. She and the orchestra engaged in a constant give and take during which her voice rose then fell to a whisper and gradually rose again stronger than ever. The audience listened in reverential silence. In the gap between improvisations here and there some spoke but immediately shut up. By the time she'd sung the whole gamut of this song's demanding variations, the singer had exhibited an absolute mastery of her art and the audience burst into loud applause.

Salim looked over the room and saw the eyes of all these men who shouted their delight and appreciation. No sooner did they sit down again than they would want to abscond with Farida and keep her to themselves. As for Salim, no one paid attention to him or had the slightest idea about his relationship with Farida. He thought he'd caught her eye. This woman with a black silhouette and an elusive smile was his wife. In an hour or two she'd remove that dress from her small body and snuggle up with him to sate her desire and claim his love. Among the horde of men there, he alone knew the complexion of her skin, the scent of her perfume and that other music she made when in the throes of passion. These stupid imbeciles would insist that the singer sit at their tables, but this woman wasn't for sale. She was married ... She belonged to one man, and one man alone.

Yet at the same time Salim wanted to scream that it wasn't him; in fact, he didn't even know this singer. His wife was a young woman who lived at Karradah and changed beds on the roof during the summer. He had nothing to do with this singer, neither as her intermediary nor as her patron. He was the husband of another woman. He loved a Farida who sang only for him. She didn't unveil in public and no man had seen her. She waited for him. He'd find her again to watch her come back to life and be with her so that together they could live out their life.

The next day Anton gloated over Farida, saying that he planned to declare her star of the month. She'd then drop out of sight, and sing only at Jewish weddings. After a while she'd return to the nightclub for a month-long engagement. He would sign her to an exclusive contract. The night before he had tried in vain to strike up a conversation with Salim. It reassured Anton that Farida said she had a patron who was her husband but he needed to play that role in public. Salim was a Jew and, therefore, didn't have the clout to carry out the responsibilities of this role.

As a young, beautiful woman, Farida couldn't say no to every man. This put Anton in a difficult position which he soon had to face when an army officer asked him to extend an invitation to the singer. He requested the pleasure of her company at his nightclub table, or elsewhere. When Anton told him that Farida was married and didn't accept any invitations, the officer immediately reacted badly. He demanded the name of her husband in order to make a deal with him. He wanted her at his table and money was no object. Anton knew that Salim, a puny Jewish businessman, couldn't stop the officer. He would laugh him off and refuse to take no for an answer. Anton had no such problems with the other singers. Men knew and accepted their fees. When he told Farida about this predicament, she just shrugged her shoulders. Did she need to remind him of their agreement? She wasn't a prostitute.

Salim came to the nightclub at the end of the evening and a taxi drove them back to Karradah. Overflowing with excitement, Farida talked all night. That turned Salim on. She couldn't sleep until she reached the point of exhaustion. At the office Sasson complained that he saw little of Salim and briefly at that. How could he make Sasson understand? He'd bring him to the nightclub. Salim lived in a fog absent-mindedly going through the motions of life. He only snapped out of this daze when in Farida's arms. If he continued to live like this, he would again wind up in a sick bed.

That evening Anton took Farida aside before she went on stage. "Your husband must watch over you," he told her. "I can handle the hot-headed young officers and minor civil servants, but those in the top brass could wreak havoc on the nightclub." He cited the example of Baghdad's singers, each of whom had an official lover. If they didn't, they spread the word about their fees. As for famous singers, Asmahan's brother had her back while Mohammed Abdul Wahab took Leila Mourad under his wing. Umm Kulthum was too old, ugly, and renowned to need a sugar daddy, though one never knows.

"I have Salim," Farida half-heartedly said to herself. He wasn't a coward but this small time Jewish merchant wouldn't stand a chance against military and tribal leaders. After all, he couldn't stave them off with his bare hands. Farida would have to protect Salim.

FARIDA

"Jawad Hachem's in the audience," Anton told her after her first set of songs.

She shrugged her shoulders.

"He's Baghdad's chief of police!" Anton exclaimed. "It's the first time he's come in person to the nightclub."

He usually sent his underlings. Anton never hesitated to compensate Hachem for his benevolence ... because in the twinkling of an eye he could shut down Anton's establishment. Furthermore, Hachem had the consideration not to make specific demands. Less greedy than his predecessors, he also set an example for his minions. Although he had a reputation for incorruptibility, one had to take this with a grain of salt.

Anton busied himself catering to his guest's every desire and that of Hachem's two lieutenants.

"You've caught a rare bird," the chief of police remarked in a conspiratorial yet wry tone.

What did he mean?

"I'm glad that our star pleases his Eminence."

A little later one of Hachem's lieutenants came up to Anton.

"His Eminence would like to congratulate Farida."

"What an honour! I will tell her."

The lieutenant didn't budge.

"We'll meet in my office, not in the audience. The poor girl's shy and fearful."

"That's also what his Eminence proposes. He does not want her to join him at his table."

"She doesn't sit at anyone's table."

"All the better."

Anton didn't breathe a word of this to Farida. After singing her second set, she went into his office to collect her pay for the week. Jawad sat there drinking coffee with his two lieutenants standing beside him. The two walked out as soon as Farida walked in.

"His Eminence wishes to congratulate you," Anton said.

"Farida, you're the Middle East's best singer," Jawad declared.

He was thin, with a thick, black moustache, big dreamy eyes, a small flat nose and a wide mouth. He laughed like a child, proved naturally charming and radiated personal warmth. Despite his uniform this young man made no show of his authority, much less convey the image of a brutal conqueror. Rather, he seemed every bit the romantic.

"People had told me," he went on to say. "But now that I've heard you myself, I know that there's no one greater."

"Thank you," she replied unabashedly.

"It's an honour," Anton said.

Jawad stood up.

"I'll come again. I don't want to deprive myself of the pleasure."

"It's an honour," Farida echoed, to Anton's delight.

Salim waited for her at Karradah. He didn't pick her up every evening at the nightclub and she often arrived home after he'd gone to bed. Normally, she would awake him to share her excitement. This continued until she ran out of energy and fell asleep. However, she waited until the next morning to tell him about Jawad's visit in order to downplay it, but also for her to absorb its implications.

"He didn't want anything from you?" Salim asked in disbelief.

"He came to congratulate me. What would he want from me?"

"You'll see. They're all the same. They've got only one thing in mind."

FARIDA

She sensed his sadness and, for the first time, his consternation and fatalism. She cherished him for not pretending that he was stronger than her. She knew beyond a doubt that he loved her and that, no matter what happened, he would never leave her.

Anton spread the news that the chief of police had visited Farida. He cunningly left the nature of that visit open to interpretation. When a military officer or civil servant requested that Farida sit at his table, Anton responded that she didn't accept invitations. But he then shut his eyes and whispered that the chief of police would come that evening, unless he had to attend to a serious matter ...

Waiters, musicians and other artists at the nightclub took it for granted that the reportedly incorruptible Jawad Hachem afforded Farida his protection. Anton saw to it that the news reached the ears of Sasson who'd undoubtedly repeat it to Salim and he in turn would bring it up to Farida.

Sasson resented that his friend had kept him in the dark and he no longer invited Salim to his home. Further, Salim didn't see his family any more because he divided his time between the office and Karradah. They knew that he lived with a woman but they didn't know who. By the same token, her uncle and aunt Agha didn't know who had made Farida "fall." Salim wanted to drop a bombshell with this secret. Yet he felt deeply humiliated that all their love for one another and all his money didn't suffice for him to serve as Farida's protector. He couldn't face down the army, the police and Bedouin tribes – a Jew had no business doing that.

Sasson saw through his business partner's lifestyle, worries and fatigue. Salim either buried himself in his work or, in a state of sudden lethargy, distractedly dealt with customers and listened with aloofness to Sasson. When he told Salim the rumour about the chief of police, Salim felt humiliated but he didn't reveal his key role in this. Right then and there he wanted to spill his guts to Sasson in order to free himself from the strange hold of his secret.

Jawad Hachem returned to the nightclub a week later. It rained and a cold wind blew. The few who passed by Rachid Street took shelter under its archways. The nightclub remained half empty. When Anton informed Farida that the chief of police had come, it made her so happy that she felt guilty. Anton alluded daily to her guardian angel. Hachem's theoretical presence kept intruders away.

On stage Farida's eyes met those of her admirer and his gentle entreaty melted her heart. Jawad gave without demanding. She closed her eyes to lose herself in singing. After finishing her first set of songs, she looked across the audience but saw only Jawad in the first row. His barely perceptible hint of a smile evidenced a mutual understanding that she couldn't deny. Rather, she accepted his compliment.

Farida perceived a Muslim policeman as a powerful brute who protected women and children. Some dark night she just had to say to him: "I'm your sister. I'm afraid to go home alone" – and he would escort her to the door. He wouldn't touch her because that would break a code of honour more binding than law. Yet Jawad was neither an enforcer nor a beast and she was married. Indeed she was intimate with one man alone to whom she'd given her life body and soul.

After Farida's last set of songs, Jawad left, accompanied as usual by his lieutenants. He had not approached her and that disappointed Farida. That night she hugged Salim tightly so as to melt into him. She lived to satiate her lover's desire. By arousing him and then offering herself completely to Salim, she sought forgiveness, appeased him and discovered anew what bound them together despite her erring ways. She considered her body insufficient to express her enthralment with desire because her love knew no boundaries. She sang before an audience that included Salim, who was physically present but mentally absent, and Jawad, who beckoned her without saying a word. He appeared all the more imposing since he didn't show off his power.

How could she tell Salim this? More to the point, how could she implicitly summon him to her rescue? She loved him and no one else. He needn't worry about the Muslim policeman. He comes just to hear her sing. Yet why did it please her so much to see him there, looking silently at her? This gaze didn't belie her love for Salim which overflowed and engulfed her. Even if she responded to someone else's gaze, it simply attested to this love. Her lean, tiny body constrained Farida because it couldn't contain the vast immensity of her love. And neither could Salim's body.

The next morning she wriggled out of Salim's sleepy embrace asking herself if she wasn't seeking excuses to leave Salim and his love behind. She no longer sang at Karradah. She came home exhausted and now associated music, as well as singing, with the nightclub: its ambience, thrills, laughter, cacophony and a crowd of faces. After each show it took her hours to relax.

When Farida walked on stage, the orchestra gave her an adrenaline fix that ignited her desire and enthusiasm. She tried mentally to block out the noise and had difficulty getting everyone to pipe down. She found respite in listening to the progression of her own voice. Little by little it gained assurance with each ascent. She resisted the temptation to respond disdainfully to the audience's disregard. If she did so she'd lapse into a deadening routine that would make her feel worthless. Singing would become a job, an occupation, a way to earn a living. When she returned home at night, Farida cuddled close to Salim and, to reassure herself, she repeated the words: "I sing my love for you; I sing out of love for you."

This moved Salim. Yet at the same time he grew used to it as a sort of ritual that gave her the strength and courage to continue. He loved her too and, not knowing where the road would lead them, he held her tight to play it safe. She remained the alpha and omega of his life, and henceforth its only anchor. He occasionally went to hear her last set of songs and fleetingly regained a sense of their good old days together. During the taxi ride home she snuggled up to him to solicit the support he could not offer her. However, he felt her fatigue, a feeling that increased his own tenfold.

She often strove purposely to lose herself in singing. Her improvisations on *ya laili* spiralled irrepressibly. While singing, she sometimes got goose bumps like those she experienced when listening to Umm Kulthum and Asmahan's vocal odysseys. She awaited such moments to remind herself why she had chosen this life path and, the second that her voice faded into the sought after silence, the audience went wild. From every corner they yelled out: "Allah, Allah," to shake off their stupefaction. She still hadn't run out of breath. She would resume the song and at just the right moment she would reduce the audience to silence so that it took a back seat as she floated on the waves of her own modulations. She would sing about the inadequacy of her love and console herself by burrowing into this song to rediscover the fullness of a lost love and an all too distant life.

Jawad came Friday evenings but never joined her backstage. She started to look forward to Fridays and kept watching for him to arrive. She addressed her song to him but he simply applauded like any other audience member.

At the end of one Saturday evening, Anton took Farida aside. Flustered, yet happy, he broke the good news to her – at least he considered it good news.

"Jawad came to see me," he said.

"When? Where? Is he here?"

"No," Anton said with a smile. "He came this afternoon. Thank heaven I was here."

"What did he want?" she said with a show of indifference. However, she quivered with joy and nervousness.

"We talked about this, that and the other."

"Ok," she responded somewhat angrily.

"He spoke about you. He's organizing a party for his brother-in-law, Hassan al Sayyab. He's the tribal chief of Dulaym. Each time he comes to Baghdad there's a string of receptions and parties. He reserves the nightclub and transforms it. You'd think it's a tent in the middle of the desert. His retinue, brothers and cousins accompany him all dressed in the traditional Bedouin aba."

To feign her exasperation Farida grabbed her veil, a signal to Anton that she'd run out of patience.

"He wonders if you could grace the party with your presence. He's not asking you to sing but simply to show up. He has a house at Sulaykh where he goes only for special occasions. His family lives in Haydarkhana. During the summer he spends his evenings on the riverbank at Sulaykh. It's warm enough to grill fish outside but the party will take place indoors."

"I'll think about it."

"Farida, to refuse would constitute the worst insult. You don't know the ..."

He almost said the Muslims but stopped himself in time.

"Yes, I do know them. I see them every evening."

"Here doesn't count. Jawad's the chief of police and Hassan has a conception of honour that we can't fathom. You realize that a yes or no could mean the difference between life and death?"

"I'm not afraid."

"You're not, but I'll take the rap. Farida, you can't refuse the honour of this invitation. Nothing will go wrong. Just think of it. Your presence constitutes the most beautiful gift that Jawad could give to his brother-in-law. Money can't buy that."

She put on her veil to mask her joy and excitement.

THE TAXI CAME FOR Farida at the end of her first set of songs. Anton would explain her departure to the audience. Although couched in mystery and evasive words, he'd leave no doubt about the identity of the high ranking official who invited her to his party. It would increase the prestige of the Al Zawraa nightclub.

This marked the first time that Farida had ventured into the Sulaykh neighbourhood. Jawad's sprawling house overlooked the river and seemed palatial to her. Men in civilian clothing stood at the entrance. Winter would soon draw to a close and then people installed fans and brought their beds up to the roof tops. This particular evening one could feel ever so slightly a warm breeze that foreshadowed summer's scorching winds. Wearing her veil, Farida entered gingerly into the courtyard. As soon as she walked in, a hush fell over everyone. Seated among men sporting traditional banded headscarves, Jawad rose to welcome her. Three rows of men filled the courtyard while women completely shrouded in black sat on chairs that crowded the covered passageways to the rooms. Sami improvised on the oud and with three other musicians performed in front of the men.

Jawad told Farida several times that her presence represented a great honour and joy for him. Would she like to rest in one of the bedrooms? What he meant by rest roused Farida's suspicions and apprehensiveness. So she said no. A chair awaited her between Sami and Fouad, the ney player. She walked on stage and removed her veil. This showed that she had rights denied to other women in the company of men. Many servants scurried back and forth between the kitchen and the guests offering them glasses of arak and trays full of *maza* appetizers.

Farida could feel the eyes of all the men and women on her. Yet to her surprise she did not find this intimidating. Unlike the nightclub, where people didn't know each other, here members of the same family comprised the audience and they knew each other inside out. As an outsider, she made them aware of their family ties through the delight and joy they experienced together and shared among themselves. She sensed tension in the air. Fouad, the ney player, stood up.

"Ladies and gentlemen," he said, and everyone fell silent. "Ladies and gentlemen, this evening we have the privilege of receiving as our guest, Farida Agha, Iraq's most popular songstress and one of the Middle East's greatest singers. This constitutes a singular honour since it marks the first time this incredible artist and star of Al Zawraa has agreed to sing outside that nightclub."

Applause rang out. Farida began her *ya laili* in a low, muffled almost monotone voice. With her eyes half-closed, she gradually lost herself in the song. She looked towards the river which seemed as distant as a dream, then gazed again at the audience and singled out Jawad's eyes, eyes that awaited hers. She picked up the rhythm, beating it out with her body. She thought she read in Jawad's otherwise serious face a gentle joyfulness hitherto unknown to her. Caught in a whirlwind of emotions, Farida also visualized Salim's face, a face that seemed not only out of place here, but beyond the grasp of these strangers and their world.

All her life she had rubbed shoulders with Muslims, but had never said a word to them. These men wearing their traditional banded head covers remained as foreign to her as Hindus or Americans. Nonetheless, they applauded and shouted with glee each time her voice rose then fell, over and over until, exhausted by its own richness, it faded into silence. But it stopped only to begin anew. She listened to the applause, took a deep breath, and couldn't wait to pick up the song once more.

Never before had she felt an audience so close to her or so completely under her spell. They followed her every move while waiting at her beck and call. Farida sensed the sway that she held over them and this feeling increased tenfold when she beheld Jawad's supplicating gaze. She could tell he would go anywhere with her and do anything for her. She had grown accustomed to Salim's muted passion and love based on his orderly life. But now she thought that she heard an irresistible call to the wild. She knew full well the power that she wielded and had no doubt that she would triumph in the end.

She saw Hassan Al Sayyab walk toward her, then hesitate. He's only a boy, Farida said to herself. His imposing voice and the daggers that dangled from his aba didn't frighten her. He remained but a timid young man who now spoke to a woman for probably the first time in his life.

When he came up to her, he bowed before walking over to Fouad and praised the musicians. Fouad credited their fine playing to Sami to whom the sheikh reiterated his congratulations. Sami in turn commended Farida. Emboldened, Hassan looked straight at her and expressed his admiration and thanked her on his own behalf, and his brother-in-law's, for accepting the family's invitation. Farida acknowledged this with a nod of the head and a formal, polite phrase. She then looked right past him as a sign for him to take his leave.

In the room stood a table replete with *kouzi*, a whole lamb baked over rice with tomatoes. Following the order of their rank, the men served themselves, each one courteously inviting the other to go ahead of himself. After the top dogs came the small fry who devoured everything on the table. Servants brought a second *kouzi*, this time for the women. They wolfed it down. Although the orchestra had stopped playing, the noise in the room proved deafening.

Farida decided that she would sing and then leave immediately before they served dessert, which consisted of baklava and *zelabia*. No sooner had the men finished eating than Fouad began improvising, followed by Mourad, the kanoun player, then Sami. When the whole orchestra chimed in, it signalled the singer's second set of songs. Standing in front of a chair, Farida opened with a series of *ya laili* in a high pitch. She abruptly ended these and started to sing, *Ala dhafaef dejla merr*, one of her own compositions, then segued into those made famous by Leila Mourad and Asmahan.

United in their enthusiasm, men and women alike exploded into applause and cheers. They had come there to celebrate and comprised quite a different audience than that of the nightclub. Farida gave voice to their joy and for some constituted its substance. At the end of her set, Farida slipped away. She was the outsider – not because they were all Muslims but because their party wasn't hers. As long as she sang, she would not belong to a family, to any family.

On her way out, Jawad met her at the door. He held her hand in both of his, then gently squeezed.

"The next time you'll come alone," he said, "and we'll throw a party for you."

She lowered her eyes and smiled, but did not say anything. A police car took her back to Karradah. Salim wasn't there. This time she felt relieved to be alone.

The next day a plain-clothes policeman awaited Farida at the nightclub. He handed her a box wrapped in cloth. To avoid Anton's prying eyes, she decided to wait until she got home before opening it. She knew it was a gift from Jawad and his brother-in-law Hassan and she didn't want Salim to see it either. At the same time, she felt bad for even wishing that he might not be home. He was but had already gone to bed. In an apparent effort to seek his forgiveness for such a thought, she made passionate love to him despite the fact she had to wake him up to do so. She only opened the box the next day. It contained two gold bracelets purchased from a Jewish jeweller. She recognized their high quality because she often admired those on her aunt's wrists.

THAT MORNING SELMAN ABDULLAH woke up earlier than usual. A Selichot preceded the regular synagogue service. The city had experienced some turbulent times. Eight months earlier Bakr Sidki had overthrown the government. This brought some relief but people wondered about the ramifications of this event and what course of action his military junta would take. The nationalists fulminated more and more against the British. The Nazi ambassador, Dr. Groba, plied young military officers with propaganda in the form of illustrated books and brochures, some written in Arabic. Nazi anti-Semitism proved quite amenable to the staunchly Anglophobic nationalists who viscerally opposed Zionism. No matter how much Baghdad's Jews proclaimed their loyalty to Iraq and denied any ties whatsoever to Zionists from the Western world, they remained Jews and therefore of dubious allegiance.

Bakr Sidki silenced those who clamoured loudest but he couldn't curb the anti-Zionist demonstrations. The Jewish community held its collective breath with the upcoming anniversary of the Balfour Declaration. It of course had nothing to do with Jews born in Iraq, or their community; however, fanatics bent on causing them trouble immediately associated Iraqi Jews with Zionists. Seddinq Shanshal published inflammatory editorials in *Liwa Al Istaklal*, and even moderate nationalists such as Rachid Ali Al Kaylani and Fadhel Al Jamali made no secret of their admiration for Germany's new master.

The hammer fell with Bakr Sidki's assassination. His death consecrated Sidki as the Jews' defender. Demonstrations increased and, like their fellow Iraqis, Jews participated. They made a show of opposing Zionism as much as virulent nationalists did. Be that as it may, demonstrators killed two Jews at one protest. The Jewish community grieved and fell prey to fear. They professed more fervently than ever their Iraqi patriotism and holed up at night in their homes. Meanwhile, rumours ran rampant.

Led by Jamil Al Madfaï, another military junta took power, re-established order, and stopped the attempts to intimidate Jews. His cabinet included well-known nationalists such as Rachid Ali Al Kaylani, and Al Madfaï himself took a hard line against Zionists, although he did not go to the lengths of those who had recently converted to Nazism. The Jewish community breathed a sigh of relief. This new government sought the rule of law and considered anti-Zionism a disruption that resulted from a lack of enforcement. All the newspapers unequivocally opposed the establishment of a Jewish state, as did the leaders of Iraqi Jews.

Everyone forgot the Abdullah affair. Salim spent day after day, then week after week in jail without ever getting used to it. On visiting days, Monday and Thursdays, his mother or Naji, sometimes both, came to Bab el Mouadham laden with packages. Salim had become the main supplier of cigarettes to both prison guards and inmates. They protected him and gave him certain privileges. Yet at the same time he made sure not to appear rich, as that would have aroused envy.

Farida's first visit overjoyed him but also plunged him into despair. Did he remain the centre of her life? Did she still love him as much as at the start? He had made too many concessions and had suffered more than his share of indignities.

He couldn't see any light at the end of the tunnel. When she half removed her veil, Salim asked himself: Would life once again offer him the gift of her body? Would he experience anew its warmth and smell afresh its scent? Would it happen while they slept? In the middle of the night? In the early hours of the morning? He still loved her madly.

"How's it going? Do you manage to sleep? Do you get enough to eat?"

Her rapid fire questions didn't give Salim time to answer.

"I think about you day and night," she went on to say and then, lowering her voice: "I love you more than life itself."

This moved Salim so deeply that he didn't know whether to rejoice in her love or lament his misfortune. He knew that as an accused murderer a lifetime prison sentence hung over his head. The Karkouklis' lawyers had set a cunning trap. With Salim out of the way and his brother dead, Abraham could finally reign supreme. He had resented Salim's partnership with Sasson, especially as Sasson had despised and looked down on him. Then lo and behold Farida shows up, assures Salim of her love and suddenly he's the happiest man in the world. He just wanted to cry.

"When can we get back together?" he asked.

He no longer held anything against her. All his resentment, anger and vengeful schemes vanished in her presence. Yet some nights despair engulfed him and he wished he had never met her.

"Salim, I can't live without you. You'll get out of here. Whatever it takes, I'll spring you."

She now sang only three nights a week at the nightclub, but performed at every Jewish wedding. Anton cut records of her songs which became hits and played on the radio. Kasr el Zehour's stations, which broadcast from the royal palace, made Farida their star. One day an Egyptian-Jewish filmmaker from Cairo invited her to dine at the Zia Hotel where he was staying. Farida had a policy of refusing men's invitations, no matter what the pretext. However, Albert Sarfati's wife accompanied him. Summer had barely begun and, even though she lived on its banks, Farida had the impression of discovering the river for the first time. After showering her with compliments, Sarfati declared that Baghdad was too small for Farida. She belonged in Cairo where she'd likely become a movie star, thus allowing her fame to spread to every Arab capital from Tunis to Sana'a. She told him she felt flattered and would think about this. She had Salim and Jawad. She simply wanted to sing. Did she lack the energy and drive to go elsewhere? The question didn't cross her mind. Her present life satisfied her despite Salim's unhappiness.

"Nothing has changed," she said over and over to him. "I love you as much as the day we met."

How could he believe her? Everything that had happened convinced him otherwise. Yet each time they saw each other, they experienced all over again the happiness of their first days together.

JAWAD PROVED THE PERFECT lover. Farida had brothers and cousins that he left her free to visit because, if he sought to play a role in that aspect of her life, it would entail keeping company with Jews. This he could not permit himself to do. Of course, because of his position, he formally received leaders of the Jewish community. And he graciously accepted their gifts. He could also allow himself a Jewish mistress and set her up in a house replete with servants and guards drawn from the police corps. However, Jawad could not publicly associate himself with Farida.

"Your brother-in-law Hassan's very nice to me," she told him one day.

"He's my brother-in-law. He loves the singer but knows that no one can touch Farida the woman."

Farida knew she couldn't count on him to get Salim out of prison.

Once or twice a week Jawad came to the house at Sulaykh, mostly in the afternoon, sometimes in the evening, though he rarely stayed overnight. All the other days Farida could do as she liked, whether to visit "her family" at Karradah, sing ... whatever. Jawad never talked about his work. She knew that, when demonstrations broke out, they made him tense and worried so that he turned to her for relief, if not reassurance. Never did he badmouth Jews. On the contrary he admired them, albeit from afar. However, the fearsome, despicable Kurds haunted him.

Jawad loved her after a fashion but wouldn't run risks for her. Farida knew without a doubt that she didn't love him, yet she enjoyed his company and the feel of his body against hers. He gave her security though she often found him childish. He had a nervous disposition that rendered him heavy-handed. Did he really get a kick out of giving orders and commands? He knew, however, that he could only get his way with her through gentleness. Meanwhile, she did everything to maintain his dignity.

After his brother-in-law's party, Jawad waited a week before contacting Farida. One evening a chauffeur came to pick her up at the nightclub. Jawad alone awaited her. Dressed in civilian clothing, he looked less imposing and more accessible.

Farida found him handsome. Although a raw, animal desire possessed him, he forswore imposing himself. Without so much as touching her, he abruptly said: "This house is yours."

Like a timid patrician, he led her through the inner garden to a door bedecked with jasmine blossoms. He opened it.

"This is your room."

It came fully furnished with a wooden bed, armchairs, a sofa with a back made of cane, and a dressing table with a huge, upright mirror.

"It's like out of a movie," Farida said to herself.

She encountered one surprise after another, whether framed photos of Jawad on the walls, rugs from Tabriz and Isfahan or bottles of perfume that filled the dressing table. He must have bought them at Orosdi-Back, she thought.

Until recently she would never have dared set foot in such a store. However, since she started singing at the nightclub, Farida made it a habit to buy all her clothes at Orosdi-Back. The closet in Jawad's house now beckoned her. He had an impish, gleeful smile that suddenly became unsure. She gave him a look that signified her approval though he knew that she would remain discreet.

"It's insane. How could you have gone to such lengths?"

"It's a tribute to you, the greatest singer, and I ask for nothing in return."

"I cannot accept all this."

She then nestled herself in his arms.

"It's insane," she repeated.

"You know that the man comes with the house," he said. "You can't chase him away."

"I have no desire to do so," she said while at the same time taken aback by his statement. She shied away from his gaze.

Farida wanted this man, but not in the same way as Salim. Salim represented the heart, the soul, love, everything. Jawad represented something else, namely, extravagance and luxury. They quickly undressed and jumped in bed. Although an introverted leader, this man of action certainly expected a lot from her. She surmised that he must have gotten used to prostitutes who pre-empted men from taking any initiative. Farida acted as if she herself wasn't a ... though the idea didn't bother her, nor did she find it shameful.

She no longer had any honour. She'd lost it some time ago, the first time she responded to Salim's passionate gaze. Since she had nothing else to lose, why not enjoy herself and drink life to the full? As for Salim, she loved only him and always would, but she had more love than she knew what to do with. Her fleeting affection for Jawad just served to prove this. Even two bodies didn't suffice because they couldn't contain her happiness, a happiness that knew no bounds. Confusion blurred everything in her mind but she felt happy. How could she experience such joy if she had done something wrong? She had so much love that her body seemed to imprison that love. She would explain this to Salim and he would understand because he too loved her.

The next morning in the dining room she found breakfast fully set out with cream, honey, and tea. The house had other occupants after all. An American woman in her sixties who cooked, and a Kurdish maid in her twenties who spoke with a funny accent.

At eight o'clock the chauffeur arrived at the front door. "Jawad had everything planned down to the last detail," she said to herself. While she admired this, nevertheless it upset her that she had so easily fallen into his trap. He stood up and looked at her not with love nor passion but rather with thanksgiving, happiness and contentment. The expression on his face reassured her. She couldn't resent him. He'd give her the shirt off his back.

Yet she knew that she would antagonize him if she did not respond in kind so as to establish a relationship of give and take. She had nothing to lose in the exchange. On the contrary, she would have two homes. Karradah offered her Salim, life, love and family too, whereas at the other end of the city Sulaykh afforded her luxury and, though she was reluctant to admit it, protection and security. Who'd dare touch her now? Jawad loomed larger than life. His name alone would ensure that no one came near Farida. The chief of police himself had taken this great singer under his wing and made her his mistress.

For him she represented the extraordinary. This beautiful,

young, affectionate woman anticipated his every wish and stood at his beck and call. Yet she did so without a hint of unseemliness. He enjoyed her company and she his body. Farida would never have imagined that a Muslim, much less one in uniform, could seem so much like the men in her family, and need her, along with her moods and whims.

She heard through the grapevine that, before she moved in, the house already had a story of its own. Jawad had received it in appreciation for services rendered. At first he intended it as a summer home for his wife and children, but they didn't have the slightest wish to leave their residence at Haydarkhana. Jawad didn't insist and instead used the house for other purposes. He initially hosted family celebrations, then friendly get-togethers for officers. Yet rumour had it that he reserved the house above all for a lady whom he invited to stay there a week or two at a time. Some spoke of a Turkish dancer in town; others mentioned a Lebanese woman. Be that as it may, the house henceforth had only one guest, Farida, who ruled the roost. Even Jawad hesitated to give the cook and the maid any orders.

Despite her patience and tact, Farida had a lot of trouble trying to get Salim to accept their new living arrangements. She now had her own house which an admirer had given her. This news so upset Salim that he fled Karradah in the middle of the night. He'd never again see Farida. A week later he returned to Karradah and, to his profound dismay, Farida had removed all her personal effects except for a few clothes and cosmetics.

Salim could no longer work or sleep. Sasson suggested that he hook up with Nadia to forget his troubles and just have some fun. The thought of this made Salim sick. He'd rather spend his evenings by himself in Karradah dreaming of

Farida and reliving their most cherished moments together. He mulled over in his mind her characteristic gestures and vocal inflections. But he refused to play her records.

One evening Salim walked through the door and found Farida sitting in her favourite armchair. He threw caution to the winds and rushed into her arms. She cried, squeezed him and ran her fingers over his face, back and arms as though to ensure herself that he was all there. She seemed to discover his body for the first time. He too cried. They stayed like this for a long time and then, almost unconsciously and without saying a word, they took off their clothes and climbed into bed. They went at it with as much aggression as gentleness and as much raw physicality as sweet tenderness. While lying on her back with her eyes closed, Farida let Salim cup her face between his hands and she apprehensively began to talk.

"I swear, Salim, I almost committed suicide several times this week. Without you there's nothing left for me. Neither clothes, nor jewels, nor money, not even singing could make me forget the angry, belligerent look on your face. I love you, Salim. There's no one else and never will be anyone but you for me. I'm a singer and must accept all that entails yet without you and your love I can't go on. If you turn away from me, I can't even sing anymore. I live or die with you."

It pleased Salim to have this time with Farida so that he could lay down his conditions.

"Drop everything," he wanted to tell her. "Let's get married and have children like everyone else."

"But, Salim, we're not like others. Give me one example of a man and a woman who love each other as much as we do despite everything."

If they got back together, it would be on her terms. He

also felt pity for her because, regardless of what she believed, she didn't have the freedom to leave the gilded cage that entrapped her. Salim had run his relationship with Farida back and forth in his mind for a week. When he took into account rationality, family and the future, everything indicated that he should make a life change. But he couldn't bring himself to do it. All his troubles and despair vanished after one hour with Farida. He knew everything about her, including the identity of the other man in her life. If she and Salim got back together, he would need to accept the Muslim and never say a word about him. Indeed Salim would have to pretend that Jawad didn't exist.

Salim knew full well that she must have a protector and that Jawad represented for her an admirer, nothing more. Although Salim knew this to be true, how could he deal with his jealousy? Must he shut his eyes to this facet of reality and focus solely on the happiness that he derived from their love? Did he have any other choice? If Farida had been a Muslim who couldn't marry a Jew, or a married woman, he would have accepted the other man in order to keep her. The misfortune that had befallen his love had only served to deepen it. Salim knew he had little time left to enjoy such happiness. He would have to snatch opportunities between the office, the nightclub, etc.

"Nor can I live without you," he said. "I tried but it's impossible."

From then on Farida completely sealed off that part of her life and, only when necessary, did they obliquely mention the other house.

"Tomorrow I'll go to Sulaykh," she said in a way that permitted no objections. And then she would ask as though to renew intimacy in their relationship and render it complicit: "Will you come to Karradah tomorrow?"

Happiness now largely eluded Salim. He stole it from the jaws of adversity for a few moments at best. Sequestered from a dimension of Farida's reality, he already felt her increasing absence and neglect.

Salim had never spoken openly about Farida with Sasson who, during the early stages of his marriage, didn't broach any subject that could perturb Najiah. Everybody knew the whole story of Salim's clandestine relationship. People kept quiet about it so as not to take sides and occasion any unpleasantness. To act otherwise would put an end to many friendships and social ties. Sasson carefully avoided any mention of Salim's scandalous life.

Word soon got around that Jawad Hachem had once and for all taken Farida under his wing. Salim could thus no longer lay claim to her. Tongues began to wag and each biting remark cut to the quick for Salim, though he always feigned ignorance, if not indifference. Out of affection for her brother and to show that she believed his romance with Farida had ended, Najiah suggested one evening, while Salim met with Sasson and her, that they go to hear Farida at the nightclub. Sasson seized the chance to invite Salim to join them. As Najiah had expected, he refused, but got her message loud and clear, specifically, that they could henceforth speak openly about Farida. However, this did not hold true for Khatoun who blocked out any talk of Salim. Although proud of his success, she had lost all hope of marrying him to a rich young girl from a good family.

ONE NIGHT WHEN HE came to pick up Farida at the nightclub, Salim found Sasson there by himself.

"I'm on my way out," Sasson said.

"What are you doing here?" Salim asked in an angry tone.

"I came to listen to the music," he responded and then left.

At the nightclub, as long as she remained the chief of police's preserve, no one came near Farida. Salim had second choice but everyone knew that he had lost pride of place and thus felt a certain contempt for him. If Farida had frequented any other men, people would have considered Salim her pimp.

The nightclub's management lost their previous respect for him and began to perceive Salim as a conniver.

Two weeks after their paths crossed at the nightclub, Salim returned late one night to Karradah and found Sasson outside his house. Farida had stayed at Sulaykh that evening.

"I was waiting for you," Sasson said.

"Has tragedy struck the family?" Salim wondered.

He and Sasson had kept their import/export business after they obtained exclusive rights to produce kosher meat. As a result they made it rich.

"I wanted to talk with you about Midland Bank's letter."

"What letter?" Salim shouted angrily. "You've chased me all the way here to talk about a letter? I just left the office."

"I didn't know. I was at the slaughterhouse."

"Did you come looking for her? It's not me you hoped to find."

"Don't get angry."

"You're a snake in the grass, an unscrupulous lowlife."

"Who do you think you are to talk to me in this way?"

"If I ever catch you hanging around here again, I'll kill you. I mean it. Leave Farida alone."

"Nobody owns Farida," Sasson said, attempting to lighten the atmosphere.

"Sasson, I'm telling you one last time. If you even think of touching Farida, I'll kill you."

"Calm down. You're speaking like a Bedouin."

"Get out of here this moment."

At their office Salim talked strictly about work and business. One evening Sasson tried to convince Salim to go home with him – for Najiah's sake, he claimed. However, Salim didn't want to see anyone. He could only relax with Farida who increasingly showered him with tender loving care.

When alone at Karradah, Salim sometimes said to himself that he couldn't go on like this. He dreamed of leaving, of pulling up stakes, of moving far, far away, where he knew no one and nobody knew him. He felt bitter towards Farida, but this disappeared as soon as they got together. Indeed he then only spoke to her of his love and joy. By the same token, she had never shown him so much affection. Did she endeavour thus to warrant his forgiveness, even though she didn't evidence the slightest twinge of guilt? Salim attributed the change in Farida's behaviour to something else, namely that she no longer had any expectations. Since declining Sarfati's offer, she seemed to have turned her back on ambition. Salim afforded her rest and relaxation. He proved an oasis for Farida. They shared the same background and she now gave no thought to the future.

Instead, she took full advantage of each moment they spent together. She readily fulfilled his every desire.

"Do I make you happy?" she asked him.

"Yes, yes," he responded.

Why would he want anything more? He sought no other happiness than this one. Yet it always seemed to keep him at bay and gave him no assurance that it would last. Why does the most satisfying moment never suffice? Does it not find its true significance in the memory and imagination which magnify and enhance it so that it becomes inviolable?

Despite his initial despondency there, the jailhouse consoled Salim. He subsequently got impatient to see Farida again. When she visited him everything once more seemed possible. She would never think of asking him if he was guilty or innocent. This question lies beyond the pale, or at least the two of them would not cast it in those stark terms.

Neither of them ever again mentioned the event that a week earlier had turned their lives upside down.

Salim had come earlier than usual to Karradah and Farida had already returned there from the nightclub. Lights shone brightly in the house and at the doorstep Salim heard a man whose laugh he recognized as that of Sasson. This paralysed Salim. Sadness, anger, and an incredible sense of helplessness overwhelmed him. So Farida and his brother-in-law, as well as business partner … He wanted to turn around, go back and walk the streets. But he didn't have the strength. He then heard Farida's voice though he couldn't make out her words. Sasson again laughed gustily.

An adrenaline rush impelled Salim stealthily to put the key into the door lock and, when Sasson saw Salim, he went beet red. He stood up and smiled sheepishly.

"Salim."

Farida called out from the kitchen: "Salim, is that you?"

She hurried out and hugged him.

"My love."

He extricated himself and, without uttering a word, showed Sasson the door. He walked out and didn't so much as look at Farida. Salim raised his arm to strike Sasson but he had already sneaked away.

Salim sunk deeply into an armchair and covered his face with his hands. Farida waited for a few moments and then in a stifled voice said: "Salim, I swear by our love and all that's holy that Sasson didn't lay a finger on me. Salim, believe me. I wouldn't let any man touch me, Salim."

Her tears flowed. Salim looked at her like a cursory, vacillating object.

"Salim, I beg you for the sake of our love, you must believe me."

Without even glancing at her he stood up, undressed, got into bed, and put one arm over his eyes.

He lay there on his back and Farida didn't dare touch him.

"I came home early because I couldn't wait to see you," she said. "I'm so afraid I'll lose you, and worse still, you've willingly distanced yourself from me."

She stopped speaking. Meanwhile, Salim lay motionless next to her.

"I wanted to surprise you by getting everything ready for tomorrow morning so that we could have more time together. Sasson had come to the nightclub with your sister. I agreed to see your business partner and his wife. They made me swear not to tell you about their visit but I still don't know why. I'll do anything to hold onto you. A week later Sasson came back alone. At first he asked me where you were. Afterwards he timidly beat around the bushes insinuating that I no longer belonged to you body and soul and was, therefore, now available ... I sent him away but not too gruffly since he was your brother-in-law and business partner. Tonight I found him in front of the house. He said he had something urgent to tell you and didn't know your whereabouts. I couldn't leave him on the street and you would soon arrive home. Darling, you must believe me."

Was the bed the same way he left it the day before? He had pulled back the bed covers too quickly to notice. He would see in the morning light if the clothes, chairs and everything else remained in place. Salim dozed off, then abruptly awoke when Farida's foot brushed his leg. He feigned sleep while she slyly played footsie. His lust betrayed him. Farida's hand slid down his shoulder, over his belly, and grabbed his rock-hard penis. Salim couldn't control himself and Farida felt anew that he wanted her. Their bodies silently fused as they squeezed each other tight to stifle words, words that lend themselves to doubt and suspicion.

Truth dwells only in the body, Salim once told her. He was wrong. The body had many features that prove as uncontrollable as the wildest imagination, and as unsure and as unreliable as dreams. The thought of Jawad made her feel compassion for Salim and pity for both him and herself. In their embrace she sought sweet revenge for the infidelity of body and soul. Farida realized that she was letting go of Salim and that he was leaving her. Nothing, not even her body, could hold him back.

Poor Sasson. What an idiot. Did he think she'd service him because of her arrangement with Jawad? Did Sasson take her for a prostitute? Although Sasson had had difficulty putting it in words, what he wanted from her proved glaringly evident. Seeing his best friend, brother-in-law, and business partner hit on her, how could Farida set Salim's mind at rest, especially since he imagined that everyone schemed against him? Could she be sure of her love when she remained unsure of her body's dictates and her heart's fluctuations?

For Salim, Jawad represented the unknown, the unattainable and the faceless. His name constituted a taboo and any allusion to his existence was deemed off limits. In exasperation Salim could leave Farida at the drop of a hat. Although she didn't have the courage to admit this and despite doubling her displays of affection towards him, Farida derived a certain satisfaction from making Salim jealous. How else would she know if he still loved her after enduring such pain and humiliation?

She could have sent Sasson packing but his almost vulgar jokes amused her. Had she shamelessly wished for a confrontation between him and Salim? She couldn't care less about Sasson. She could put him in his place at any moment. However, Farida wondered if Salim slowly but surely assumed the role of a consolation prize. Had she mistaken an ingrained habit for faithfulness, and obstinacy for profound feelings? Did he make her happy? In any case, nothing devastated her more than his absence. As for Jawad, he brought her enjoyment, exquisite sensitivity, pleasure, support and security. He proved a helpful happenstance, but not a necessity. She sang to keep herself centred. Her singing echoed a new unease, and the same old sadness.

One evening Salim arrived at the nightclub before Farida had finished singing her set. He felt impatient and hopeless as though he had come to the end of his rope. What did she keep hidden from him? Part of Farida, and her love, lay beyond the pale for Salim and that idea marginalized him.

At the office he now threw himself too much into his work while at the slaughterhouse he wore a sterile, frozen smile. The day after they met at Karradah, he clenched his teeth and told Sasson, right there in the office: "I've warned you. I'll kill you if you ever do that again." For the employees who witnessed the feud Sasson tried to downplay it by smiling lamely in response to Salim's threat.

Out of fear Sasson asked himself if he mustn't get Najiah to intervene. Yet how could he explain showing up at Karradah? Najiah spoke about finding a fiancée for her brother. Farida represented but a youthful fling that had gone on too long. All men sow their wild oats.

In any case did not Farida remain untouchable? Jawad had many resources at his disposal. Sasson would wait a few days before telling Salim that this all amounted to a misunderstanding. He never had any intention of hitting on that woman. To boot, she didn't even like him.

However, Salim's attitude had hardened and he turned a deaf ear to Sasson. Salim adopted a strictly business approach. One week later they arrested Ismaïl Hassan with a dagger in his hand and blood splattered on his clothes, while Sasson lay dead in a pool of that very same blood.

When Nouri Al Saïd succeeded Jamil Al Madfaï at the head of government, the Jews breathed a sigh of relief. Word had it that this Kurdish, albeit thoroughly Arabized, prime minister would bring an end to uprisings by Kurdish tribes in the north, and rule the army with an iron fist. But most importantly, that he, though not openly favouring Jews, would protect them from the nationalists' dangerous extremism. Some of its leaders reminded the Jewish community that Al Saïd had studied at the Alliance Israelite Universelle school and that he held Jews in high regard. Nobody knew exactly when he studied there but this rumour reassured everyone.

The new government put its words into action. The administration stopped harassing Jews so they could once again walk the streets in peace as well as hold big wedding engagement parties, and bar mitzvahs. Moreover, Jews could now come home safely late at night. Nevertheless, Seddig Shanshal and Faïek Al Samarraï continued to write diatribes on behalf of Palestinian nationalists. Nor did they hide their admiration for Germany's new master of ethnic cleansing.

Grief enveloped the country one morning when it learned that the night before the young king Ghazi had died in a car accident. He had mounted the throne six months earlier following his father Faisal, a friend of the Jews and adored by them. He had signed an agreement with the Zionist leader Chaim Weizmann and a photo of them together graced the living room of many Jewish homes. Immature and reckless, Ghazi proved indifferent to Jews. Unlike his father who socialized with some prominent Jews, Ghazi apparently cultivated no friendships in the Jewish community. Word got around that he covertly sympathized with Germany and that he advocated Iraq's developing nationalism, including the blatantly pro-Nazi version.

Hearsay had it that in his many palaces he had led a decadent life of drinking binges and numerous lovers. Indeed a Jewess apparently counted among his favourites. Even if true this would not prove, much less ensure, that Ghazi harboured a soft spot for the Jewish community.

The news of Ghazi's death shocked the Jewish community and struck it with fear of the unknown. Every sudden change triggered anxiety among its members. Anything could happen and that included a takeover of the government by those who made no secret of their animosity toward Jews. Meanwhile speculation about the causes and effects of Ghazi's death set tongues wagging. The authorities saw to it that photos of the accident scene and wrecked car appeared in print but the gossip continued unabated.

Most attributed this incident to the hidden hand of the English on whom people frequently laid the blame. Rumour had it that the almighty English often worked in the shadows. Whether the Kurds rebelled or the army mutinied, it boiled down to the English. Cornwallis, the High Commissioner, proved a deviant in the disguise of an ambassador. He pulled all the government strings and condemned the young monarch to death because the English proscribed his Germanophile and Anglophobe tendencies. Others pointed to the dark side of the young King's life: alcohol, womanizing and his latest vice, automobiles. Contrary to court customs and rules, Ghazi himself was driving when he crashed into the tree. He had just left the arms of one mistress and was on his way to another's house, perhaps that of the Jewess.

Abdul al-llah would serve as regent until Faisal II came of age. The Jewish community maintained that Abdul al-llah's friends included some of its members and that he had no sympathy for Nazis. Nationalists considered him a yes man for the English, while Radio Berlin's Iraqi mouthpiece Younes Al Bahri, labelled him a lackey and considered his uncle, King Abdullah of Jordan, a traitor.

Abdul al-llah's hatred of Nazis reassured Jews that he would not hassle them. Life returned to normal and people could once again calmly walk the streets at night in peace.

Nothing that he read in the newspapers gave Salim the slightest indication that his circumstances would change. As a prisoner he couldn't expect the government's overthrow to result in his release. Neither the status of Jews nor the tasks of policemen had changed in the least.

During her last visit Farida seemed worried. The nightclub had closed for the period of national mourning. However, before leaving she repeated as usual: "No matter what happens, you won't stay stuck in here."

He believed her since he had no choice.

When Farida moved to Sulaykh, she considered herself a guest who awaited the master's visits. Her own home was that of her beloved at Karradah.

The house at Sulaykh already had occupants, specifically, a cook, maid and alternating two-man police detachments that watched over the chief of police and his home. Although Jawad had handed Farida its keys, she waited a long time before giving any orders in the house. Be that as it may, her work at the nightclub had taught Farida to assert her wishes while Salim's arrest made her aware of her loneliness as life passed her by. She went regularly to Karradah. Did the cleaning lady keep the house spick-and-span? Only at Karradah did Farida feel at home. With Naji she took care of Salim's business affairs because he knew that if found guilty the authorities would put all his holdings under lock and key. He set up a checking account in Farida's name and she weekly deposited his money in it. She carefully kept track of all his accounts. As the testimony incriminating Salim piled up, Farida worked out her strategy and tactics. In the hope that she'd convince him otherwise, he told her that they would find him guilty; however, she no longer made light of such fears. Instead, she simply stated that he wouldn't go to prison and left it at that. The mystery surrounding this affirmation grew ever more impenetrable.

Since the house at Karradah ceased providing a place for passion and relaxation but constituted only a hasty stopover, Farida began for the first time to take a hard look at the Sulaykh house. Jawad now came there only once a week and rarely spent the night with Farida. Had his love cooled or did he tell the truth when he said he had too much to do?

At first the guards, Fahim and Sadeg, tried to show each other up when watching over Farida, but as time went by and Jawad's visits tapered off, they left early in the evening so that she found herself alone with the cook and maid.

Although born in Nasseriyah, Fahim lived with his wife and three children at Kadhimayn. He would lay down his life for Jawad. The sun had furrowed Fahim's inscrutable face, a face which initially scared Farida. Sadeg, the other guard, lived with his wife and two children in her parent's home at Bab el Sheikh. Despite his frail appearance he proved strong and resilient. However, his furtive gaze unnerved Farida.

Anissa the cook gave all her earnings to her widowed 30-year-old daughter, who raised alone her two children. A worrywart, Anissa nonetheless proved herself determined and very generous. The Kurdish maid seemed somewhat stupid, but Farida came to realize that she didn't lack intelligence; rather, Arabic remained a foreign language for her. By pretending that she didn't understand she could get away with many things otherwise forbidden. Farida caught her unveiled in conversation with travelling salesmen and delivery men. "She'll end up in a bad way," Farida said to herself, without knowing exactly what that meant.

One day Fahim arrived late. Why did he live so far away? He couldn't afford the rents in Sulaykh. So Farida decided to offer him the house's adjoining shed which served as a storage room near the river.

She told Jawad what she intended to do and about her fear in his absence. He immediately gave his consent. Since they no longer needed Sadeg, Jawad assigned him to traffic control. When Farida rode to the nightclub and passed Sadeg on duty at Bab el Mouadham, she made the taxi driver slow down so that she could greet him.

When Jawad mentioned that his sister needed once again to find a maid, Farida jumped at the chance. She had no use for Jamil who actually got in Farida's way. The cook sufficed, and if necessary, Fahim's wife Zahra could lend a helping hand.

FARIDA FELT ALONE. JAWAD sometimes spent a couple of hours with her but due to anxiety and exhaustion he did little more than kiss her and drink a glass of arak. Then, perhaps out of a sense of inadequacy, he sheepishly returned to his wife and children. Meanwhile, Farida had nothing more to prove at the nightclub where people gave her standing ovations even when she sang without feeling. Despite this, she completely wowed the audience, which caused her to feel disdain for them. She needn't worry; Jawad and Anton both had her back. Furthermore, she answered to no one. She tried not to think about Salim. She had told him that Sasson never touched her, in fact no man … Salim knew it; yes, he certainly knew. So they dropped the subject for good.

Farida could no longer clearly visualize either Salim's face or his body. When she awoke each morning, she stared at his photos, as though he had vanished without leaving a trace, except for those pictures. She ceased to recollect Salim. Indeed her visits to the jailhouse brought back memories that seemed to her far removed from the defeated man who now pinned all his hopes on her.

Salim professed his innocence but his words rang hollow in the face of facts and testimony that grew ever more incriminating. Office employees who had previously grovelled before him recounted trifles that the presiding judges, prosecutors and courtroom audience ate up. Witnesses claimed they heard Salim say that he would kill Sasson, while the murderer daily added new details indicating that his boss had masterminded the whole thing.

Farida handled Jawad with kid gloves so as to detect any telltale signs. Despite her mental readiness and willpower, Farida's body no longer obeyed her. Instead it went AWOL. Salim's memory sucked the life out of her and brought Farida to a standstill. Her melancholy singing ostensibly conveyed an emotional honesty whose proof she sought in vain. Since she now went on automatic pilot when singing, it became an unbearable lie. Farida loved Salim because she needed him. She loved Salim because he gave her the breath of life, the impetus to sing, and carnal desire.

Anissa spoke about her daughter's widowhood with Farida. Did Anissa do this on purpose? If the cook perceived Farida's heartache, then others could, too. Subterfuge no longer concealed her despondency. Furthermore, Anissa talked about how much her daughter also physically felt her husband's absence, although she never admitted it to herself, much less voiced it.

Anissa forced Farida to eat, arranged her clothes, and pressed them. One day, when she found a freshly ironed dress on her bed, Farida told Anissa: "It's no use, I'll never wear it. Give it to your daughter." Farida had come to loathe material things and detest colours. She took it out on her dresses and shoes.

Every day Farida put assorted dresses, skirts and undergarments on the bed and told Anissa: "They're for your daughter." Farida remained convinced that Anissa didn't watch over her for selfish reasons. Material things couldn't buy her. She protected Farida the same way she would want to protect her daughter.

One day Anissa said: "This dress would look very good on Zahra." Did Fahim concern her? Did Anissa seek to defuse his jealousy by harnessing Farida's generosity for his wife? To her surprise, a week later Farida saw Zahra wearing one of her dresses while she dusted the furniture. "I'm helping Anissa," she maintained.

"I don't need help," Anissa yelled from the kitchen. "I've shouted my lungs out repeating that to you."

"Let her do it if it makes her feel good," Farida ordered.

Zahra went back to work. When Farida came out of her room, she gave Zahra a handful of candies.

"For your children."

Everyone would soon take her for a paragon of virtue and munificence. The next day Fahim stood at Farida's front door and wouldn't budge.

"What do you want?" she asked, puzzled.

"Ms. Farida is the most generous woman I know."

"It's nothing. I wish Zahra and the children health and happiness."

"Dare I ..."

"Go ahead, Fahim, I'm listening."

He recounted a long story about a cousin in Nasseriyah who had lost his wife, had a child, was a policeman and wanted to marry Zahra's sister in Baghdad. Farida grew more and more impatient as she awaited the upshot of Awni's troubles and aspirations.

"I'm afraid to ask Master Jawad, but Awni would like a transfer to Baghdad. If you put in a good word to Master ..."

"I'll speak to him."

She never asked Jawad for anything. However, requesting a favour for one of his Muslim subordinates ...

A week later Awni joined the jailhouse staff as though an invisible hand had shepherded him right there. That same day the prosecution summoned its witnesses to testify in court. For two weeks the Karkouklis' lawyer took wicked delight in methodically marching them before the bench. One after another Salim and Sasson's employees attested that Salim threatened to kill his brother-in-law. Through his cunning interrogative techniques, the lawyer intimated that money lay behind the murder and that Salim had embezzled a fortune because of his insatiable needs. Meantime, Salim's lawyer emphasized again and again his client's alibi, namely, that he wasn't present at the crime scene. Yet nobody had accused Salim of himself wielding the murder weapon. Rather, he chose to bribe a hapless employee who kept repeating the same defence, that is to say, Salim threatened to fire him. He had a soft spot for Sasson and considered him a model employer. However, the employee desperately needed money and Salim, a spendthrift, held out the prospect of unlimited funds.

Everything pointed to Salim's guilt and Farida had no illusions about the fateful outcome of this trial. One by one she assembled the pieces of the puzzle like a blind person feeling their way around an unknown room. She mentally would play out the moment when she would set the plan in action. She sleepwalked through it, as though having an out-of-body experience. Not for a second did she envision herself once again in Salim's embrace because her yearning would have clouded her judgement. She proceeded with unwavering methodicalness. While singing one night, a part of the plan she had not foreseen suddenly came to Farida. Her life had found a purpose. She now served a higher cause and must prove herself up to the task.

At the end of winter Farida gave orders to clear the house from top to bottom: beat the rugs, air them out on the roof, empty and clean the closets, etc. Until this point nobody bothered in the least about the basement, but now Farida had it outfitted as a cool, safe haven, she claimed, from the sweltering heat of July and August. Farida furnished it with a table, three chairs, a lounge chair, a stool, a sofa bed, and both an electric and an oil lamp.

"The master will enjoy the coolness here during heat waves," Anissa said.

Farida looked at her with uncertainty but didn't say a word.

"You've thought of everything," Anissa added. "It only needs a stove and dishes to serve as a fully-furnished apartment."

Farida again took a long hard look at Anissa who wore a complicit smile while she stared down Farida.

THE NEWSPAPERS STOPPED PUBLISHING even a few lines about the ongoing trial. Salim stood guilty in the eyes of the public and, although Jews followed this case, they appreciated that the press ignored it. The newspapers instead focused on singing the praises of the boy King Faisal II and his uncle Abdul al-llah. Their photographs held pride of place in offices and stores. The renowned poet and veteran of WWI, Maarouf al Rasafi, exceptionally published a poem that extolled the boy King's virtues. Further, the press reported his every move so much so that it paid no attention to the nationalists. Nuri al-Saïd, a Kurd who from youth had cast his lot with the Arabs, now ruled supreme. He brought peace to the streets but gave little thought to peace of mind. Meanwhile, Jews went about their business with renewed confidence and Salim amounted to nothing more than an incident best forgotten.

Jawad relaxed more when he visited at night. He had already spoken about putting a telephone in the house at Sulaykh so that they could contact him in case of an emergency. Farida remained suspicious of this talking machine that lay beyond her control and which served blindly as a spy to sound the alarm. Anton had a telephone at the nightclub and complained that he no longer had a moment's rest nor time to himself.

As calm and peace returned to Baghdad Jawad stopped thinking about emergencies and the telephone. Some evenings Farida could hardly keep herself from spilling the beans. Since he was her elder and guardian he would understand. Besides, he liked Jews – or at least he didn't hate them. Forgetting that Farida belonged to this community, Jawad sometimes blurted out how smart such and such Jewish businessman was, or how astute a certain Jewish civil servant was. Yet Farida remained separate and distinct from Jews, in a class by herself, since she represented his lover, as well as a singer. In Jawad's eyes she could do no wrong, and for good reason: the more Farida missed Salim the more she showered Jawad with tender loving care.

Indeed she anticipated his every wish with a nurse's clinical attention and a sister's affection. The preposterousness of the latter made Farida laugh. Jawad normally came at night with his chauffeur. Although in charge of the city's security and head of its entire police force, Jawad didn't have the foggiest notion about Farida's scheme. Its audacity heartened her and banished all her fears. This powerful man would never lay a finger on her.

Jawad now and then visited Farida right after he left the office to catch a breath of fresh air on the balcony. Or so he said. Anissa offered him blackberry juice the moment he arrived and Farida stood at his beck and call. He usually caressed her arms to remind them of their past, yet still latent sensuality. For the time being he claimed it was too hot to sleep together. Someday she would tell Salim about these early evenings with the chief of police and the nature of their relationship.

"I miss you terribly," she told Salim during her weekly visits to the jailhouse.

When the hot winds blew in the afternoon, Farida stretched out on the bed in the basement. The humidity pulled a fast one on her because at first it seemed refreshing but that disappeared once she got used to it so she had a ventilator installed underneath the entry to the staircase. This let fresh air in and enabled her to see the comings and goings of both the watchman and cook. Meanwhile, she could hear every footstep of those upstairs.

NEWSPAPERS BROUGHT TO HIM by Farida reported that the concession of the Chehita had been entrusted to the Shaikhli-Karkoukli Association. Salim's name would no longer be mentioned. The cost of kosher meat had unexpectedly soared provoking a number of demonstrations in front of the community offices. A calm Hakham Bashi promised that he would make sure the concessionary would not unnecessarily boost prices during the coming year.

In a month everything will be forgotten, Salim told himself. Abraham will be filling his pockets more than before. Sporadic, fleeting demonstrations were marginal: a sign that there was no pressure from the outside. If Jews felt threatened, they would have no time to worry about the price of meat. Next year, Salim told himself, it would be good that Karkoukli disappear, that Karkoukli's name lose itself in the dark. Salim smiled at his own recklessness. Next year, he would not be in the race. He was no longer a competitor. In a week or two, the courts would announce the verdict. They would declare that he was guilty. Even his lawyer could not find a glimmer of hope for his client. He would try to lighten Salim's sentence. Instead of life imprisonment he might get 15 or 20 years. Did he know what that would entail? Having no fresh air, no trees, no anything.

He had to react, especially when Farida was around. At times, he would get upset that she should be free, that he should feel like a sick man who was jealous of the healthy around him: each filled with energy, appetite, and sleep. When he saw Farida, how he felt ashamed for experiencing unspeakable emotions. He was happy to see her, and he told himself that one day followed another, that time existed, that hope was a light that brightened the day. She was relief, solace, and especially hope. She had planned everything in advance. All he had to do was to wait for the surprise, the reward, as would a good, obedient child. She was aware of being monitored by the police and prison guards, so she could not share her plans with Salim.

"You will be getting out of here," she told him. "You will not stay here. I need your help. Trust me."

She was enjoying making decisions herself. She loved him, yes. She did not doubt it one bit. She expressed her love with her body. Without him, she was incomplete, crippled. But she still controlled this body of hers. She would take hold of herself when he would be back again by her side.

The judge would no longer be convening him. The witnesses had appeared, the defence rested. All there was to do was wait for the verdict.

One more week and his fate would be sealed.

"You will be back home by the end of summer."

Farida was his only, his single resort, his last link to living.

His mother and Naji's visits were becoming less and less frequent. They had abandoned him, certain that he would never come out. His mother's vigour the past year was kindled by stupid ambition and blind greed. Naji was rich and successful: a true provider. His mother's one and only love was Naji. In spite of the modest future waiting him, he at least would not dishonour the family. At first fascinated by Farida, Naji later fell under his mother's influence.

"A singer!" Farida was a singer who was a prostitute but who was not considered a prostitute. It was not easy to have to go through her in order to make ends meet. This salary of shame and disgrace was dwindling more and more. Soon this source would run dry. "This woman" would keep everything for herself, while this poor man would be locked up in prison for life. It was all for Khatoun, Salim thought. It was a way to exonerate himself by accepting his soul as being barren and changing it into a virtue.

The morning they brought in the verdict, Salim was relieved. He had slept peacefully, dead to the noise and heat. Like the day before an examination, he could think only about the results, no matter what these results could be. In the waiting room, he recognized Farida, behind her veil. Sitting to Naji's side, his mother.

His father would be reciting Psalms and Selichots at the synagogue. There were no doubts in his mind when the judge pronounced the sentence. There was no surprise: life imprisonment. No one would take his life away. Ismaïl Hassan, the murderer, would not be hung.

A life in prison. He could not tell the difference. He knew that he would not be sentenced to hanging. Everything was possible. As though awakening from a happy dream, he saw himself spending his entire life in a prison. A living death. He managed not to collapse. His lawyer claimed that he would appeal the judgement.

The instant he climbed into the prison van, accompanied by two policemen, Farida, face concealed by a veil, ran up and whispered to him:

"You won't stay in there. I promised you. I'll send you a parcel tonight. Don't open it before tomorrow morning."

He was losing his breath. He dreamt of a pillow into which he could bury his face. In the dark he would let the suffering climb within. There she was, Farida, mysteriously rushing about.

Resolute, Farida had only one thing in mind: the moment. She had to get the machine working. Life would unfold normally, without hindrance.

Appearances are safe. From Jawad to Khatoun to Naji, no one would doubt a thing. The judge could decide if Salim would go to prison or not, while they waited for the court appeal. The prison's list of inmates was unending. It would be months before his case would get to court. Lawyers were able to reassure their clients that they would not be moved to another prison.

It was all costly; the residence attached to the prison was itself expensive as well. Too exhausted to guide his lawyer, Salim hoped for a miracle, instigated by Farida. The lawyer was being paid by Farida, and got into the habit of consulting no one else but her. By respect but also for fear of Jawad, Salim was discreet in regards to this man of honour. She asked for a transfer which would come about two days later – in the morning.

Friday night, Farida performed as usual. Anton was thinking of shutting down the nightclub and reopening instead during the summer as an open air *malha* in Battawiyeen. He joyfully welcomed Farida's good humour during her set, singing without complaining about the heat and the lack of audience. When, the morning after, Farida noticed Fahim coming up to her, she told him straight out: "I need you."

Fahim waited, standing without moving.

"It's nothing important," she said. "But I need you. You are a serious man in whom I can totally trust. Tomorrow morning my cousin, Salim, will be transferred to the central prison. Ask your brother-in-law, Awni, to make sure to accompany him. If he will not be assigned to a different prison, he might be able to negotiate the whole thing with a colleague – even if it costs him some money. Before Salim goes to prison, I would like Awni to bring him here. It's half an hour. He'll wait outside. Then we'll be on our way. No one will suspect a thing."

Stupefied, Fahim could not find the strength to confront her.

"Not a word to the chief. I don't want to bother him with this story of no significance."

"However," Fahim replied, "even if Awni were to succeed, he might not be alone."

"He must succeed. He owes it to you. Must you remind him?"

She looked annoyed. Fahim realized he was upsetting her.

"It's nothing. A quick visit, no one will find out. I will show you my gratitude, to you and to your family as always."

Farida got to the prison, handed one hundred fils to the guard so that she could visit Salim outside visiting hours. Salim looked dazed, as though he had already found his place as a prisoner.

"Salim, you must get hold of your intelligence and energy in the next few hours. Here are my instructions. And here's a parcel. Put it with your personal effects. Respect my instructions. Or everything is lost. We will both be destroyed."

Salim coiled up in a corner. The other prisoners left him to himself. He was lost to them, condemned. He would no longer be the pusher of cigarettes and candy. The others kept away from him, as though he were a pariah. Especially as his crime, known by all, was not considered noble. He had hired a poor Muslim to kill his brother-in-law, and because of money.

He had all the time in the world to read the instructions. He then tore open the parcel: a woman's veil, and a pair of shoes.

By night, Fahim visited Awni. Chance helped. It was he who was to help transport the prisoner to jail, along with a newly hired driver who came from Mossoul. Awni had no objection in doing what his brother-in-law asked. Besides, Jawad might very well be the one invisibly pulling the strings. In the morning, Salim was sitting in the van. Awni gave the new driver the directions on where to go. Raouf did not know the city. At Sulaykh, Awni began to yell: "Idiot. This is not the road."

"It's you …," Raouf started to say.

"Me what? You're the driver, no? Do you have any idea what will happen to you if I expose you? Ten years."

"But it was you …"

"Me? Me what? I have not said a word. It is you who are the driver."

Upset, Raouf started to beg.

"Tell me what has to be done."

"Wait, you idiot. And don't you go anywhere."

Fahim was waiting in front of the house. Veiled, Farida stood in the corridor.

The day before she had suggested to Anissa that they visit her daughter. She had given her, as it was her habit, clothes which she did not want. Anissa was grateful and walked away. Fahim was left with the house at his disposal.

Awni opened the door to the van. Salim stepped into the house.

Raouf did not know a thing about the commotion. He was lost and was going to pay dearly for his mistake. So much rested on Awni. This was not the right time to hit him with a ton of questions.

"You know what to do," Farida said sharply to Salim.

"Yes."

"Step on it. And watch out."

He walked back out, towards the van. He opened the door and slid inside. Then a bang echoed in the darkness. Farida let out a scream.

Awni and Fahim began to run. Plates tumbled down in the kitchen, breaking in fragments. Farida held her foot in her hand.

"It's nothing. Why are you there? Go. And fast."

Anissa, with a veil, was standing at the door.

Farida cried out: "Anissa, you're there already?"

Awni turned the key in the lock and the car took off at full speed.

Farida put five dinars in Fahim's hand, twice his monthly salary.

"For Awni and you," she said. "Thank you. Go back home now. I need to rest."

She waited for the sound of the steps to fade before she opened the door to the basement.

Salim still waited under Anissa's veil, her shoes in his hands.

"But you're barefoot," said Farida, laughing as she went downstairs.

"Woman's shoes. They don't fit!"

She hugged him, kissed him.

"You're here. You're here," she kept on repeating.

Salim could not understand, could not be happier. The only reality, this body, so much wished for, seemed all of a sudden so small, tiny, which he hugged blindly, avidly, without his spirit being part of his actions. Farida undressed him, and then undressed herself.

"It's you, Salim. I'm Farida. My love."

He obeyed his body as though he were an automaton. He would end up recovering it, finding his flesh again, discovering Farida. The odour. It was her odour.

In her eyes, this big man in her arms was her sole love. She tried searching for his body and her own body, watching in exasperation with all of her being the love that she had kept for so long buttoned up within.

She would imagine him, with neither face nor body. But there she was, holding him in her arms, this body, this arm, lips that did not correspond to the image she had of them in her dreams, did not put an end to her impatience. She repeated: "My love, my love, my only love," just to silence her disappointment.

Salim was shorter than the love she felt for him. He pulled her into his arms, but she moved back while still caressing him, her fiery hands no longer obeying her will. What was escaping her was not desire, but the code of desire, the wait for her rebirth. And it was with relief that she heard the footsteps in the room above their heads.

"It's Anissa. She's come back. The real one."

Farida moved back some more and nervously laughed, as she freed herself. Salim stared at her, his eyes dazed.

"Fear nothing. Now that you are here we will concentrate on every step, every gesture."

"But …"

Fear had to be tossed aside. Life was scampering back in. Farida found a confused Salim looking for his lost dignity. Soon, he would be himself again. She would find her man.

"We are two of us, my love. Together, we'll fix everything. We are back together again, inextricably bound."

Alone in the basement, Salim stared at the walls. Decorated. Carpets. Photographs. Farida. And more of Farida, the singer. At the start humidity left him with a sensation of coolness. A ray of light filtered through the basement window with its view of the outside staircase. It would be through that window that he could see the comings and goings of people. During summer days the room was bathed in darkness. He heard someone walking in the room upstairs. He told himself that it must be Farida. Light, quick steps. Anissa's footsteps were heavier, without surprise. He turned on the fan, and lay on the bed. Every five minutes he looked at his watch. Ten-thirty, ten thirty-five, eleven. The clock clicked but time did not move forward.

In prison time was sliced into slivers: wake-up calls, meals, awakenings, meals, curfews. Screaming, laughter, snoring. He listened for noise from the outside. Sulaykh, before lunch. No fruit peddler, no pop seller, not even a car. The space was deserted. A lost house. The world vanished so that he, Salim, could find his breath again, and Farida's skin and fragrance.

He was shivering with a sense of plenitude that he'd never felt before. He now understood what it meant to miss Farida, total emptiness.

Farida shuffled from the kitchen to the room, jumping with joy, victorious. Salim was there. He would leave no more, would never leave her. She would waste no time in communicating the secret of her happiness to Anissa, whom she viewed with affectionate condescension. She had no idea what would happen in general – or what would soon happen specifically to her. For she was now deep in the story. Like Fahim, like Awni. She wanted to tell Anissa everything. That they were the protagonists of her happiness. That they were setting a prisoner free. That they were giving a man back to his wife. In the evening she would sing. She would sing about her happiness and her impatience. He would be there always, waiting for her, waiting for her to come back home. Everyone would keep the secret. She had not given them a choice. Their lives depended on it.

THE STORY MADE THE front page: both newspapers – *Al Bildad* and *Al Zaman* – reported the news without editorial commentary:

> *Salim Abdullah received life sentence, outwits his guards. The police are on the look-out. The investigation has begun.*

Al Istaklal went further: "The Jewish criminal left no trace, except his shoes. Has he a good reason to ridicule our police force?"

Awni opened the door, called the driver over.

"Come and see, you idiot. What have you done? You've let the prisoner escape."

Raouf repeated the phrase without getting it: "The prisoner has escaped."

"What are we going to do?" Awni yelled.

"What are we going to do?" Raouf repeated.

The police and the guards turned in circles around them.

"We left the prison and drove straight here," Awni said, looking at Raouf.

"We left the prison and drove straight here," Raouf repeated.

"Raouf knew the road to take. I shut the door. Lock and key."

He lifted his hand indicating the key. They tried the lock. They slid the key into the lock. No trace of a breaking and entering. How could the prisoner have escaped?

When they notified Jawad, he got angry and then shrugged his shoulders.

"A Jew. Could we prevent a Jew from escaping?"

A point of esteem we associate with slyness and irony made him forget his anger. Luckily, the criminal was not dangerous. A story of Jews. It would not instigate trouble with the Kurds and the Talkefs. He passed the investigation on to a colleague who normally spent most of his time drinking tea and coffee, instead of moving about working.

Tahsin paid a visit to the Abdullah family, inspected their house, and asked Salim's father, mother and brother questions. Back at the office, no employee could add anything more.

He asked Najiah who, wearing a veil, did not stop weeping. He had heard of his association with Farida. But as she was his boss' lover, he realized he was treading on dangerous ground.

Newspapers no longer mentioned the incident. A week after the escape, another event came to the fore and claimed headlines:

The Germans invade Poland. World War II has been declared.

Salim learnt in prison about warmth. During the first days of his escape, he thought only about love and desire. Having found Farida again, she would now fill his mind.

Salim offered himself a freedom given to him by another, a new sort of freedom that required nothing from him. Nor did it demand action of any sort. All he had to do was wait patiently for what was to follow.

"I'VE GOT TO GO downstairs," Anissa said one day.

"No, don't you dare!" Farida exclaimed. "Why?" she then added, pretending to be indifferent.

"I sometimes hear noises," Anissa said. "Rats are having a ball down there. It's been weeks since I cleaned the basement."

"I cleaned it while you weren't here."

"You? Why?"

"Because I had the time to do it."

She was unable to hide her embarrassment. Anissa didn't understand. Or she preferred not to.

"Anissa, there is something I must to tell you." Her voice was quivering, her eyes flickering.

"Yes?"

"Better for you to know. Salim Abdullah, whom you've heard about, is hiding in the basement."

"The killer?"

"He's innocent, Anissa. A victim of a trumped-up charge."

"Ah? You've spoken about him. I know nothing myself."

"You can believe me. I know him."

"You're the lady of the house."

Anissa turned to go to the kitchen.

"Yes, I know. It's dangerous to have him here. Especially

for his sake. For us as well. If they find him, we're lost, even if we're innocent, even if we were to scream that we were unaware he was here."

"It's you who knows," Anissa whispered.

"You too, you must know, Anissa. You were here when he came. You are here today ... Even if you declared your innocence, the police wouldn't let you go."

Anissa covered her face. She had tears in her eyes.

"Weeping won't help, Anissa. You are my sole supporter. You could help me, like I would if you needed me."

She held her arms, tightly.

"All will be fine if we keep our mouths shut. One must learn to keep a secret. You must tell no one."

Anissa raised her eyes, looking at Fahim's home.

"He is totally involved," Farida said. "It is best if he keeps his mouth shut. He doesn't know anything yet. But I will let him know. Together we will succeed. Salim won't be here forever. He'll soon be gone. He'll be forgotten. You'll see. Everything will be fine."

Anissa smiled thinly, and sighed.

"Mr. Jawad must know nothing. Especially him. No one. With your help, Anissa, we will all be safe and happy."

When she went downstairs that night, she found Salim caged like a lion. His eyes were different, accusing.

"No use moping," Farida said, containing her anger. "I do what I can."

There was no one else. She was not forced to risk getting killed for him.

He took her hands into his, lifted them to his lips.

"Excuse me, Farida. I sometimes get the impression that I exchanged one prison for another. It must be the heat. I'm ungrateful. You are my joy. What else do I need?"

"Everything will be fine," she said. "You'll see. It will not be as hot today. Soon summer will be a memory."

One afternoon she did not want to go down. Fahim was there, recounting his children's latest pranks. Farida waited for the right time to announce Salim's presence. But Fahim just kept chattering. Then the door to the basement opened, and Salim's head popped out.

Farida waved to him, motioning to go back downstairs. Fahim, however, had noticed him.

"Come on out," she said, as though she were talking to a child. "Now that you're there, come on out." She turned towards Fahim.

"You know Salim. It was you who brought him here. Now he doesn't want to go again."

Farida laughed nervously.

"What do you want me to do?"

Fahim was floored, dumbfounded.

"I could not denounce him. I was thinking of you, your family, cousin Awni. You will end up in prison. Perhaps you might even get killed. Imagine. Policemen organized a prisoner's escape, a prisoner who had received a life sentence."

Lit by daylight, Salim had a stupid smile.

"But the master," Fahim stammered.

"He knows nothing. Fahim, you're an intelligent boy. You know he must not be told at all cost. Otherwise, he might get us arrested. Me too. What would be left to do is to repeat what happened myself. I was facing a *fait accompli*. You and your cousin are at the door, with the prisoner, refusing to go, mobilizing the neighbourhood, even if we don't have neighbours nearby. Lucky you."

Fahim looked at her eyes, raised his head and then lowered it.

"Myself, I feel my life is in danger. But my only worry

is you, Fahim. You and your family. It is about your own security. The fact can't be disputed: the prisoner is right in front of you."

Fahim nodded in agreement. He was the policeman to whom his superior gave orders. All he had to do was to carry them out. He could not figure out how he was responsible for this story. Farida had forgotten that it was she who had asked for this service. Why would he now be the cause of this commotion? His wife? His children?

It felt like Farida was reading his mind.

"As for Zahra, it is best that we tell her nothing. The less she knows about this the better. In the meantime you work as usual. I will take care of the rest. If there is something else, I will let you know."

Automatically, Fahim clicked his heels against the floor, lowered his head, and sauntered off.

"You acted like a madman," Farida said to Salim.

"Farida, when you don't come down, it is worse than receiving a life sentence. You know what it is like. You don't need me to tell you this."

"You are an escaped prisoner. You know what that means. Your life is in danger, and so is mine. I let Anissa in on it. I was about to tell Fahim everything, when suddenly you appeared. It's done. But I beg you, don't make a false move. Our lives depend on it."

He smiled, and sat down near the entrance, at ease.

"What are you doing there?"

"Now that everybody knows …"

"What if someone were to knock at the door?"

"I would have time to run downstairs."

"You're impossible. Be careful, Salim."

He jumped to his feet and embraced her.

"Not here, Salim." She freed herself, and in a gentle voice

added: "Downstairs. I'll come. We must take our time."

She waited for the evening before leaving, and barely had time to get ready for the malha.

Anton noticed another modification in her relationship with the public. Her self-confidence bordered on indifference. She toyed with the audience. She did not open up comfortably. There was no sign of impatience in her singing, no sign of expectancy. This was a quiet stroll without incident. She did not want to forget; she did not want to free herself.

When she came back from the malha, she could not fall asleep. She stood outside on the porch. The breeze was cool. Autumn was around the corner. Soon it would be winter. She heard the door to the basement open. Salim rushed up and embraced her. She held him tightly.

"Come to bed," she whispered.

They would finally enjoy the entire night together, as they had done in Karradah.

She woke him up early.

"You have to go downstairs."

"Why?"

"Anissa will soon be getting up."

"She knows."

"It's best she does not see you here."

This was no time for protesting. It was she who was afraid.

He needed time to get used to this arrangement. He was making progress. Every day, every week something new appeared. The vice grip would gradually be loosened. He didn't think of freedom. He needed Farida. This was superstition. He had lost his sense of responsibility. Being a prisoner meant he lost his free will. He was living with air-conditioned despair. Soon he would be a prisoner no more. He might become a fugitive. Or something worse. But this was something else. He had done nothing to his guards. He had let himself be used. The time would come when he would have to start thinking about the future, about projects to come. For the time being, he needed to rest. He needed to pull himself together.

Then one night the alarm was set off. A car stopped at the door. Police in uniform stood in the front of the basement window. For a second Salim thought they were coming for him. He heard the door and footsteps in the room above. It was Farida. And Anissa. Then heavy footsteps hammered against the floor. That was Jawad. This had to happen. Salim couldn't catch his breath. He lay on the bed, and listened to the noise above. The steps moved outside to the porch. He heard Anissa busy in the kitchen, and then running to the porch. Again he heard footsteps. Farida and Jawad. They were making their way to the bedroom. The noise was chaotic.

"They are undressing."

Then silence. Salim was sure he was losing his mind, lost between the anger of powerlessness and despair. He felt he should climb upstairs and chase this evil man, and shoot him with his gun. He noticed the policeman shuffling outside his window. He had to be patient. The silence was becoming unbearable. How could she? She said she loved him.

If he could, he would have invited women to the house. He would have made love in front of her. But now he was in her hands. She could humiliate and ridicule him. He would not let himself be used much longer. He would die from it. Too bad. Again he heard noise. The monster was leaving.

"May he die. May lightning strike him down. May he be shot down. May his car crash."

The door shut. Salim. propped up on his bed, began to weep. Like an animal in a cage. What he needed was to give up his life. He preferred to kill himself rather than go back to prison. He had to overcome this ordeal. He had to avenge himself. Everyone would learn that he was a man.

Farida appeared. He wiped his face. She cuddled up to him, gasped.

"Don't cry," he said coldly. His anger subsided. He would be comforting this woman as he would a girl caught red-handed.

"No use crying."

She brushed her face against his chest: a frightened pet searching for protection. He would not be softened. Yet he knew. It had been a century since he had known. Jawad, the master of the house, became an involuntary host. Why lie to ourselves? He was a powerless victim. He would be crying about his fate. He straightened himself. Farida pushed him, and stretched beside him on the bed. She caressed his forehead gently, as though she were trying to rock him to sleep. He had no desire to undress her. Yet his passion pulled him. They rested one beside the other without touching. What did she want? His forgiveness? He was too weak to offer his forgiveness. His acceptance? He had no choice. Of course, it was death or life imprisonment. And she ...

He stood up. Farida's eyes began to glow. Gentle. Sly. Expectancy. She got up. She undressed him. He held her against him, removed her nightgown passionately. He loved her. He could not control his love. He could curb his passion, counter his impulses, but he had no power over his love. He kissed her. His kisses and fingers travelled over her skin wishing to erase any trace of the monster, of his traces in the night. A young, fresh, all offering woman, who loved him. They gently discovered their bodies, subjected themselves to the orders of their flesh, searching in the caresses for a way to give birth to what the miseries of day and everyday life had soiled. Their bodies burst with ardour, triumphing over what they had suffered and would suffer.

"You must go downstairs now," Farida told him, without much conviction. "Anissa …"

"She knows that I am here."

"So …"

Anissa did not know that Salim was Farida's lover, her one and only man. But she would soon find out. Farida wanted to scream her love to the world, proclaim that her love was alive, that she was living this love fully.

"I want to keep you, my love. I want you in my bed forever, beside me, every single night, throughout my entire life."

She was going to join him that afternoon, bringing him newspapers that she had asked Fahim to purchase for her. *Al Zaman, Al Istaklal, Al Raï El Am* and the *Iraqi Times*. In the evening he would leave his hiding place, step out onto the porch, and stand in the shadows. The breeze grew colder. "Soon winter will be here," he told himself.

She would be coming back from the malha. He was impatient, and in love as if it were their first night together. She had but one urge, to slide into bed with him. She told him about the world as she saw it. Outside: Anton, the officers of the malha, the Regent, the rumours, the government. He corroborated her news with what he had read avidly in newspapers. Nouri al Saïd had been in power for a couple of years. He did not hide the fact that he was an ally of the English. No one alluded to his Kurdish origins. He was an Iraqi, the strong arm of Iraq, the man of circumstances, the man of the hour. He was able to keep the nationalists under control. He made concessions by accepting Rachid Ali Al Gaylani in his cabinet. Nouri was no friend of the Jews, even if as a child he studied at the Alliance Israelite Universelle school. But there were rumours floating about. Rachid Ali was a nationalist too, a friend of the young warriors squad. He belonged to an old family and had links to the tribes. He was not openly hostile to Jews, as was, for instance, the Regent, Abdul allah: a weakling people considered sly. Younes el Bahri's voice heard on the Arab radio programs from Berlin sounded more and more triumphant. They mocked the British for their defeats on every front. The Germans progressed with their march to victory. Czechoslovakia, Poland, Norway, Denmark, Belgium, Holland, France. Soon England. Rommel's legions were liberating the Arab lands one after the other. From the gates of Cairo and Alexandria, they would soon be knocking at the gates of Damascus and Baghdad.

Al Istaklal alluded to the dissensions within the cabinet. Without naming Rachid Ali, it hinted at his becoming the spokesperson for the nationalists who demanded Iraq's neutrality.

Salim got into the habit of sitting by the river and reading newspapers all morning long. Farida would wake up late, especially after her shows at the malha or a performance at a wedding. Becoming the superstar of many Jewish families, she was being asked by people to appear at events as a part of their dowry. Thirty dinars when she came after her performance at the malha and fifty dinars when she did not sing at the malha. She knew families, had acquaintances, appreciated the value of dowries. Yet she was an outsider in spite of being Jewish.

People were happy to welcome her as an artist, though she was not a woman like other women. Of course, men would not dare take liberties with her, as they would do with dancers, be they Christian or Muslim, slipping dinars under their bra straps or under their belts, fingers hesitating, making sure the bills were firmly fixed. During extravagant weddings, aside from the normal orchestra, there would be one that played occidental music, a jazz band, playing for the few dancers way into the night. Not only was she the most important artist there, their national singer, Farida, but there were also two or three famous dancers. Farida looked at men getting excited, titillated by the presence of women, forbidden but not banned.

All that was needed was the cost of paying for a rendezvous. No one did. Serious and solemn at the office, these clients turned into adolescents, forgetting their spouses and their families not present. Men took saucy liberties. They knew that after the soirée they could saunter quietly back home to their lawful wives.

Farida detested these men. Salim had taken many risks. He chose not to have a hearth of his own, not to establish a home. He chose to leave the fold. She recognized in her man, a partner and a companion, the only person deserving of her love. She preferred Jawad to these men who dreamt only to slip a bill under the strap of a dancer's bra.

Salim waited for Farida to return to the terrace. He walked to and fro around the house. With the neighbourhood in deep sleep, he boldly walked down to the river. One evening, Farida surprised him standing outside. She was about to reprimand him but let herself be pulled towards him, his hands over her mouth. He invited her to take a stroll. She trembled with excitement at these stolen kisses, at re-discovering the birth of their love. They were alone, alone yet together against their families and society.

On certain nights at the malha, Farida became exasperated by young Nazi apprentices yelling, bursting with laughter, recounting the exploits of Hitler's armies. She would become impatient with the childish games of the Jewish husbands.

She wanted to rush out and meet with her true love, Salim. A short man who was putting on weight, who had nothing to say, but who would expect everything from her: stimulation, comfort, refuge.

Just as she was about to push him away, she calmed herself. She let her sweetness mix with Salim's sweetness. He was submissive and dependent. He would find tenderness later, once he freed himself of his elation. He would find his woman, his only love, his eternal love.

Exhausted, they would sleep late into the next morning. She would wake before him, studying him in detail. This was her love. Curled up like a caged animal, he was ready to run away at the slightest noise.

She would grow soft, maternal, a protective older sister. Love appeared like a responsibility, a weight. Where would she find freedom? A singer, she was a prisoner in the malha. Jawad's woman: his lover, his prisoner. She was a prisoner of self-pity. Salim opened his eyes. Farida melted in his sight. She loved him. She would always love him. She had only him; he was her possession, his total freedom. She snuggled up to Salim. She began in broad daylight their night embraces. She felt Anissa watching over her. She would have to warn her if ever Jawad ...

NEWSPAPERS NO LONGER SATISFIED Salim.

"Everyone owns a radio," he told Farida.

Means were not lacking for her, but she lived in Jawad's house. They needed an antenna on the roof. She would have to mention it to him one day. Jawad stared at her suspiciously.

"Why? You're not interested by politics."

"No, but politics are amusing."

"Do you want to listen to your records on the air?" He was being ironic.

She became quiet. In fact, her voice on the radio bothered her. She did not even recognize it as her own. Not to be able to recognize her own voice troubled her. In action she could be a stranger to herself, as she was as a recorded voice. At times, she surprised herself talking alone, waving her arms, moving across the stage, listening to herself sing; it was all unbearable. By becoming conscious of herself, she broke the spell, snapped the magic. She found comfort only in Salim's arms, forgetting everything, finding herself, loving him.

Jawad visited her less and less often. She complained. She was serious: without him, she would be lost. He had become more important now that Salim was living in the same house. Listening to her complaining he answered that he was too busy. A smile lit up with satisfaction over his face. This reminded her that a war was being fought along the borders of their country. Jawad spoke of Rommel's contingents with enthusiasm. But if she asked a question, he would not answer. He distrusted her. Feeling that she was being rejected, she took and caressed his hand. She tapped into his vivacity again but he would not reveal more than he had to.

With the coming of the month of March, Rachid Ali took over the government. Jawad grew calmer.

"The British are lost," he would repeat. "No one can stop Hitler."

Farida was confused when the mention of war rose between them. It was his turn now to speak of the radio.

Montgomery's men were backtracking. The Eighth Army was lost. Wavell and Glubb Pasha would soon be swept away. Jawad started to become a man of marble. Even his walking had changed. His attitude became military, his voice victorious. His long-term dreams did not include Farida. She had no place in his future.

"Pity we don't have a radio here." No sooner had he pronounced these words than he changed topic. He asked for a glass of water. He regretted saying what he had said.

The following day, Farida gave Anton the task of buying a radio and installing an antenna.

While in each other's arms, Salim and Farida listened to Radio Baghdad. Then it was the radio from London, Berlin, and Bari. In Berlin, Younes Al Bahri, an Iraqi, was ridiculing King Abdullah, and threatening Abdul al-llah, mentioning the miseries awaiting the Jews in Baghdad. When Jawad noticed the radio, he smiled, then frowned.

"I did what you asked me," Farida told him, her arms enveloping him.

"It was I who asked you?"

"You've already forgotten? Perhaps you'll come home more often, if I no longer suffice."

He was too happy to get into an argument. The night before, Rachid Ali Al Gaylani had become Prime Minister. The nationalists had come to power. He expected neither change of job, nor promotion. Being at his apex, he would not move. No one knew better than he the intrigues that already soiled the communists, now with Jews and Christians, even with a Shiite from Najaf here and a Kurd from Zakhou there.

A few weeks before, the Minister of the Interior had contacted him. In the presence of a British officer in uniform, he had to reveal in detail what he knew about the CID, the secret police, which he officially supervised only partially. His dislike of the British grew in him. He blushed with anger and shame. With Rachid Ali in power, change was in the air. He listened to the news on the radio. Then followed announcements and greetings from sheikhs for the new government. Tribes were uniting. Kurds were uniting as well. The Assyrians could no longer count on the French, as had been the case in the North years before. The government would not declare war against the British. Neutrality: this was all he wished for.

Hitler had no need for the Iraqi army to win the war. That they were in cahoots, that yes! Rachid Ali could ably move about. He used soothing terms, even permitted violent emotions within the army and the masses to burst out in the open in newspapers. Farida was there, standing close to Jawad. Had she explained the situation to him? She did not share his point of view. Though she had left her family, she was still a Jewish woman, one from the Jewish people.

She might be cumbersome. But it did not matter. Even the worst kind of nationalists would understand that a man could use a Jew to satisfy his needs and desires. He would not disappoint her. He looked at her. As he had never done before. Coldly. Distantly.

"I will never leave you," he said, excusing himself. He felt he could read her mind. "Never."

He felt an urge to go to her, something that had to do with fidelity, a past loyalty. His desire arose from some memory, the memory of love that could replace love, that could become the substitute of love. A memory that could be as powerful as love itself.

She was alone, afraid. She needed this man to protect her love. This was her man. She felt a sincere affection for him. Born out of gratitude, out of guilt for having lived a clandestine existence, without his being aware of it. She wanted to smile. This man knew every secret of the state, every secret uprising, and yet he knew nothing of what was happening in his own house. She caressed his hand, the hair of this man who looked like a boy who had not experienced the evils of adulthood.

As soon as Jawad knocked, Salim would run out, hiding in the woods, near the river. Winter and summer. He could not stand being near the other man. Coming back, he would find Farida, tame her, re-discover her. "Rachid Ali is a Nazi. You'll find out. His is an evil government, it will be no good to the lives of Jews."

Farida tried to reassure him. He was scared, but needed to warn her. Poor boy. When she was ready to return home, she would feel her need, the only need she ever felt, this need to lie beside him and together wait for sleep to come. But Salim was there, watching her every step.

"What do those at the malha think?"

This question became a ritual. During her absence, Salim stuck his ear against the radio. He came up with a rational analysis of the news transmitted by London, Berlin, and Baghdad. Hitler was invincible. Inexorable. He was pushing forward. Soon he would be here. Maybe catastrophe would bring Salim some sort of salvation. He did not expect anything from Farida. She had used up her financial resources. Now, faced with these events, she had become powerless. He was not upset with her, for he was as powerless as she was. The future for the Jews was darkened with evil and uncertainty. In his hole, he was not even a Jew. He was a fugitive. That is, a nothing. It was not even a question of love. Yes, they loved one another. "Love is lived in the present tense," he told himself. From day to day. However, love ran up against the limits of what is immediate.

"What do those at the malha think?"

No one needed to hide their joy, or silence the screams of triumph. The British had been defeated. They had succumbed to the attacks on every front. Soon Hitler's frontlines would reach Baghdad. They would quickly meet his enthusiastic allies, engaged in their manoeuvres, before even appearing on the streets. Rommel was the lord of the land. Soon he would be swarming his way on Rachid Street. Farida was terrorized by the victorious roar of young military men, bureaucrats, and certain sheikhs.

She would have to lessen the horror of the news to Salim. His fear, his lack of power, paralyzed her. She was upset that he was there, inactive, scrutinizing her with lost eyes. As though she was responsible for the ways of the world and Hitler's victories. He was hanging onto her, throwing words at her that changed into pricks and jolts. All she had to do was to listen to him and say he was right. Whom could she confide in? She had no one. Jawad? If she lied and used her tools of seduction. He came to see her out of habit. She knew it. She tried hard to hold him back. Without being aware, nastiness about Jews popped up in his sentences. She became moody, swallowed her shame. He wanted to direct her to another subject. She was becoming annoying, and she knew it. But she knew that all she had to do was excite him sexually. When she spoke of his successes, he became animated, filled with enthusiasm. He was loyal to her. If she betrayed him, if she dishonoured him, he would seek revenge: savagely, barbarically, blindly.

Fortunately, Salim was there to bring her back to life, back to herself. In the shadow of a tree, Salim waited. Despite her warnings, he would multiply his mistakes. As though he were fighting against some evil spell. There was an invisible enemy who allowed him to act freely only one gesture at a time. He wanted to live dangerously. He wanted to feel the blood flow in his veins. She directed him outside. She hugged him. He was a few millimetres taller than she. He expected deliverance, closure. Was this love nothing more than this? A short man who counted on her? Who needed her good will? She stepped back inside, certain that she would be there, always, waiting for him, expecting a gesture to happen. He had nothing to say, except to repeat what he had heard on the radio or what he had read in a newspaper. He bombarded her with questions.

What are the officers saying? What is Anton up to? As if it mattered. He belonged to her. He was her possession. Without her, he would be lost. The past few days he fearlessly walked to the river, wearing a kouffiah, his face almost fully covered. She was not happy with herself for feeling pity for him. She was his protector. She could give him orders on how to behave. But when she was not there, he would slip out of her control. He would break the limits of prudence. This is how he gradually distanced himself. Yet he maintained a closeness that enabled her to see him without totally taking hold of him. When he had been in prison, she had dreamt of spending such moments with him, caressing him, and he caressing her, loving and being loved back. She had never imagined him small, incomplete. All he had to do was take a few steps away from her, and she would happily chase after him.

As the days passed by, their audacity grew. In the evening when Farida would not be singing at the malha, she would cover her face with a veil. He would wear the kouffiah. Together they would stroll by the river.

Jawad did not invite anyone anymore to Sulaykh. Everyone knew that his house had become the home of the woman he protected. The government of Prime Minister Rachid Ali Al Gaylani was getting ready to receive the German troops. People listened to Radio Berlin where Younis Al Bahri and Amin Al Husseini, the mufti of Jerusalem, announced the defeat of the British. They condemned the British sympathizers, the Regent King Abdullah, the Jews, the Zionists. They promised them all the most terrible vengeance.

Rachid Ali's style was that of an old-fashioned nationalist, which seemed less flamboyant than the nationalism of the young followers of Nazism. Every month, he would convene the heads of the police in Liwa, a neighbourhood in Baghdad. After heated debates, he would beg them to keep their eyes open and not tolerate petty criminals, without elaborating in any way. Calm reigned nevertheless. Violent incidents were rare. The wait was calm, trusting. One evening, as Jawad left the office, the Prime Minister asked him: "It seems you own a house in Sulaykh."

"Yes, I do, your Highness."

"We're neighbours."

Rachid Ali lived in a *kasr*, a modest palace, or rather a large house, by the river. Salim and Farida had made this house the limit, the boundary of their outings.

"I walk by your house every day," Rachid Ali admitted.

"It is yours, your Highness."

Jawad weighed the Prime Minister's remarks. Was he alluding to Jawad's double life? But he was a one-woman man. He had a single friend, a lover. It was public knowledge. Was he expressing his hostility to the fact that Jawad's lover was Jewish? Never had Rachid Ali given into the Young Nazi movement. Perhaps he wanted to purchase his house? Perhaps inspect it? Without thinking, Jawad let out: "I would like to organize a party in your honour. Would you consider blessing us with your presence?"

"Next Friday?"

"It would be an honour."

Jawad was overcome by happiness. But, when he started thinking about the details of the event, his face turned into a frown. Farida would not feel at ease. She could be the evening's artist. Everyone would know that his lover was Jewish. Perhaps the Prime Minister was aware of this. Not that Rachid Ali was known for being anti-Semitic. He supported the Arabs' claim in Palestine unlike any other leader before him. All she had to do was leave.

One evening, Jawad waited in his car outside the malha. Farida feared the worst. She put on the smile of seduction.

"What joy to see you. Why did you not come in? You don't want to listen to me."

"Yes, yes. But I was in a hurry. I'm going to drive you home."

"Are you staying?"

"Unfortunately not."

On his face there was clearly joy. Farida was reassured, continued: "You don't have time for me anymore?"

"You know I do," he said, feeling guilty for not sharing his joy. "I'm organizing a party in honour of the Prime Minister."

FARIDA

"I will launch my new song."

"It's that ... it's that ...," he mumbled. "I don't think the Prime Minister ..."

Farida understood. The lover, Jewish on top of it, was not going to be part of the ceremony.

"I won't be there," she said, tightening her lips, reacting with relief and anger.

"I knew you would understand," he said, without setting eyes on her.

They did not speak, and neither he nor she dared break the strange new code.

Once in Sulaykh, Farida feared for Salim's life. But a solution appeared like an illumination. On the evening of the event, they would be in Baghdad. Salim would be wearing Anissa's robe and veil. Anissa had a single wish: that Salim get out of the house before Jawad's policemen. For Rachid Ali's visit, there would be increased protective measures. There were many foes. The British machinations could be efficient as well as unpredictable. That evening Farida and Salim, wearing Anissa's veils, were on the road to Baghdad. He was able to be there, appreciate its streets, its houses, its stores, the faces of the city. Never had Baghdad disclosed in him such a multiplicity of impressions: Kurds and Jews on the streets, the neighbourhood was not foreign to them! Enormous, unending city. Walking beside him, Farida was silent. He found in her attitude the happiness of their first days together, their first encounter in El Saadoun Park.

Men, women, and children filled the streets. He did not count the endless procession of men in aba, kouffiah, oriental attire, speaking, laughing, not worried about being overheard. Never had he seen this city. He was laughing inside. This was the city in which he had been born. It should have been the only city he knew, and yet he realized that he had never looked at it before.

"Let's go to the souk," he said.

They had time to waste. He needed to find a place to hide until the next morning. He never thought for a second that one day he would be able to walk beside Farida in the souks and not be recognized. Here were the shops of Daly, Rahamin, Rabic. Familiar faces were concentrated on the task at hand. There was no stopping, no absence or departure. Imperturbably they showed their patterns, boasted the quality, haggled over the price, measured sizes, money dropping into pockets. What a spectacle. Life was on the move. Salim wanted to scream his joy. He wanted to share this joy with Farida. But she was a shade. She walked on without speaking. People might have recognized her voice. At the souk, they asked that material be set aside. She spent, she spent. Waiting for a client, there stood Sasson's cousin, eyes alert. He did not like Sasson but he would eat Salim alive if he could. Salim slowed down.

"Madam, I have some beautiful fabric," the man said, taking Salim for an elderly Muslim woman. Salim frowned. He had not paid attention to Sasson before, too preoccupied as he was with himself, lawyers, and the trial. But Sasson no longer existed; gone forever.

Salim wanted to stop at a café but decided not to. He was accompanied by a woman, and he himself was dressed as a woman.

"I'm tired," Farida said.

There was a bench on Abou Nouas Street. It was the end of winter. Salim looked at the boats, the round kouffas, admiring the skilled fishermen in their movements. He remembered his summer trips on boats with Sasson. He frowned. He stood, and said: "Let's go to Ghazi Park."

They took Abou Nouas Street and soon found themselves at Battawiyeen, in front of the house he used to live in. What had happened to his father? His mother? Naji? He never asked Farida anything about them. Before she organized his escape, she had told him: "Your goods are safe."

What was left to do?

Farida did not keep count. She handed money to lawyers and policemen. Salim had been given room and board for months. He felt like laughing, sharing his laughter with Farida. Fed and Bed. Luxuriously. One day, who could say, he might in turn buy and offer her lavish gifts.

"I'm exhausted," Farida said.

Where to go? Salim was scared of being caught, if ever he stopped. They were two women strolling through the labyrinth from souk to souk. What could be more innocent? These two women could be mother and child, walking along Rachid Street. Nothing abnormal here? Two women in a café? In which café? At the cinema? Some could take them for a prostitute and her pimp waiting for the next client. Two women could not stay alone, without a man, without protection.

Farida felt alone, abandoned. She could not share her fears and tears with Salim, who expected everything from her. Without her fame, she would be an unmarried Jewish woman, without a family, the target of violence, the object of lust. She was walking on the streets, a homeless drifter, with her lover, a fugitive from the law.

Farida had reached the limit of her strength. She paused by a barouche.

"Let's go to Sulaykh taking Ghazi Street," she said.

This road stood out in this miserable city. It crossed a number of alleys aligned by newly dumped debris left by the neighbours. Past Bab et Sheikh, they moved on east to Shorja. Then Henouni, the poor Jews' ghetto.

Salim had the strong impression that these roads were lined with hiding places. From windows hidden eyes scrutinized him, ready to denounce him at any moment. He had stepped into the heart of a hostile city. Men and women spied on him. The emissaries of an implacable authority were on the lookout for him. To his side, Farida, indifferent to his misery, did not speak. Rightly so. She would willingly hand him over to the police. She had enough of seeing him in front of her every day being scared. He did not have more protection than this disguise that could only temporarily trick his enemies. In prison he could not see clearly. He had waited. Now, he had nothing to wait for. He had become a weight of no importance on Farida. He did not cherish the idea that he had to thank her. She had saved him by getting him into another prison. All for love. Where had love gone to?

He could imagine her under the veil. His desire for her was rekindled. They crossed over the dirt-covered alleys down to Sulaykh. With all her money and celebrity, Farida was now as powerless as Salim; she the poor Jewish woman in an inhospitable sea of Muslim police and soldiers chanting Hitler's victories.

The carriage drove along the street passing a lit house where stood the police and soldiers.

"Stop," Farida screamed, when they reached the dark alley that brought them to a neighbour's house. She paid the fare, and waited for the coachman to turn back before alighting.

They made their way to the river, walking under the date palm trees where they paused a while before ending at the malha. Become silent shadows, they peered at the night, their home. A commotion awaited them. No, they had not been caught. The earth began to shake, the city trembled. A short man, sidara on his head, came out accompanied by soldiers and civilians. Jawad was there. A car switched on. A door shut. There was a guardian, a policeman and the chief's car. Soon Salim would have to leave the house, and Farida would have to leave her hearth.

The house freed, Farida pushed a sleepy Salim ahead. Without uttering a word, they dropped on to the bed. Salim fell quickly asleep without brushing against Farida. She could not fall asleep; anger and sadness were consuming her. This shapeless mass was her only love, for which she risked getting killed. He could do nothing for her, not even hold her tightly.

Jawad would leave her, would have left her already, had it not been for her generosity and dignity. He had to give himself a good role which would satisfy his vanity. A small man, whose stubbornness could take care of his weakness. There was no doubt in her mind. He should be able to receive a reward of sorts. Was he not putting his life in peril?

Farida was his salary for danger, his payment for fear. She wanted to push Salim away, demanded he go. He had to leave her alone. She gradually dozed off.

At dawn, Salim went to sleep in his room downstairs. He felt a sense of well-being in being alone, in having the bed all to himself, to be the master of his space. Before going to the basement, he had glimpsed Farida. Her face was tense, her hair tousled. She had never been so sombre. When he held her tightly, he refused to look into her eyes. He wanted to avoid this revelation. Where had the Farida of El Saadoun Park gone? He imagined her face under her veil, a tiny woman, dark-skinned, with black hair. He would have asked her to remove the colour in her hair if he could. Decadent. His life was in a woman's hands. How could he admit to himself that he did not love her, that he no longer loved her as he once did?

For a week, they avoided one another. They would eat together, would listen to the news on radio, but at night, as though obeying a tacit command, Salim crawled back to his hole, where he spent hours awake before slipping into a recalcitrant sleep.

"What an adventure!" Salim said, hinting at their escapade.

"I was scared," Farida said. "I often thought about Sasson."

"So did I," Salim said, half mockingly.

"He was so young, poor boy."

"He was my age," he said, irritated.

"But you are here, my love. Luckily."

"I am here, but I belong to the world of the absent."

"You know, on the evening that you surprised him in Karradah … I want you to know. He never touched me. Not even with a finger. His pretext was you. Had he touched me, I would have thrown him out."

She spoke rapidly.

"Why are you telling me this? And why now?"

"Salim, it's like you did not grasp it. But it changed my life. Mine and yours."

"I know. Since we've come down to secrets and settling accounts, it was not I who killed him."

"That's obvious. We caught the killer red-handed. I wonder what pushed him to kill."

"Do you want to relive the trial?" he said.

"Don't get upset. I simply want to understand."

"Everything has been said. There's nothing to understand."

The next day she came back with more questions.

"Did he have a family, Ismaïl Hassan?"

"What does it matter? I don't know."

FARIDA

They were reminiscing about the first days of their love. Salim changed topic when nostalgia threatened to grow into accusations and regrets. He was unable to look at life in the past tense.

"The present is a prison," he said one day, and laughed.
"And me? Am I not the present? What about the future?"
"Poor Farida. You deserve another man, another fate."
"I'm not complaining."

ONE EVENING, AN ANGRY Jawad stepped into the house silently, as if not wanting to be noticed, as if hiding. Salim barely had time to escape downstairs.

"Jawad, what's happening?" Farida asked.

She wrapped her arms around him.

"Didn't you read the newspapers? Didn't you listen to the radio?"

"Not today."

"Rachid Ali has stepped down. The British don't want him there. They've put another man in his place. Such is our freedom, and such the independence we sing about."

She wanted to tell him that she was neither the enemy, nor his adversary. She wanted to tell him that politics did not interest her. She could only think of her own fate, Salim's fate, and the fate of the Jews.

"Who is the new Prime Minister?"

"Taha al Hachimi."

She did not dare ask him who this man was. She stalled before finally asking, frightened: "What about you?"

"Me? I'm stuck in this place. They need me. All governments need the police. Besides, Taha is not an evil man. Such are the unacceptable circumstances of his entrance into power. Rachid Ali has all the country behind him. We can't punish him as a teacher would punish a student."

"Do you think he'll do something?"

"He's no school boy," he said briskly. "He's not a crazy adventurer. He'll teach young officers to wait patiently for the right moment to strike. I know him. He's a mature and astute man. He'll get them all."

He stood and defied the invisible foe standing before him. He moved to Farida, wrapped his arms around her.

"Thank you for being here. You're beautiful. Will you be going to the malha tonight?"

"Yes."

"There will be a lot of people. Men need to talk."

And then, as if speaking to himself: "I need to be careful. Eyes are fixed on me. They can't wait for me to make a mistake. The chief of the police has no friends. We have to let the storm subside. I'm not a politician. Rachid Ali will return. He'll get them all."

As soon as the car drove off, Farida rushed down to the basement. She spoke to Salim of Jawad's consternation.

"Who is Taha al Hachimi?"

"He's an anti-Semitic. He might be less anti-Semitic than Rachid Ali is, but they share much in common. They both hold us in their hands."

"What is going to happen to us?"

"The British are losing the war. They will try to save their bits and pieces. Hitler has Europe under his thumb."

"What is going to happen to us?" she repeated, exacerbated, tears in her eyes.

He held her in his arms.

"Farida, nothing will happen to us. As long as we stick together. As long we are the two of us together. Nothing."

She raised her eyes to his. She was unsettled.

"I would like to believe you."

"Taha al Hachimi is no worse than Rachid Ali. There's Hitler, and then there are the British."

Salim read the newspapers avidly. He listened to the radio. He did not know if a change of government would bring a change for him. He had become a ghost. Without a legal identity. All he knew for sure was that Taha al Hachimi was not the avowed enemy of the Jews.

His fate as a ghost was bound to the fate of his community, if ever he decided to finally walk out of the shadows.

The rain sunk the city in puddles and mud. For a couple of days, men and women would not go out. When the storm came to an end, the cold wind still kept people behind doors. Salim went out for a breath of fresh air for a minute or so.

With Rachid Ali gone, Jawad was able to change his lifestyle. He now got into the habit of visiting Farida in the evening before returning home. He would accompany her to the malha. He was not afraid of being seen in public on Rachid Street with his Jewish lover. But he never spent a night with Farida. Anissa made tea. He enjoyed a slice of cake, curds, jam. He then would go home without putting a finger against Farida's skin. Farida continued flirting with him, but in vain. Jawad looked more and more like a defeated man, a player who had not hit the target.

After his departure, Farida ran to the basement just to find a sulking Salim who was incapable of taking his hands off her. He held her in his arms, and in spite of himself he fulfilled his tasks in order to pay his debt. Farida became impatient and walked out abruptly. He did nothing to hold her back. Would she go as far as to denounce him? She was as lost as he was. But she would come back docile, begging him if not for affection then for his presence. After performing at the malha, or a wedding, she would join Salim huddled in his hole. Something was going to happen, he told himself, even if he had to provoke the event himself. Things could not continue as they were.

In the month of March, Jawad, as soon as he returned to Sulaykh, started to use his newly installed phone. He was speaking to Rachid Ali. At first, he wanted Farida by his side. She questioned him on the ex-leader's health.

"He's doing well," he said helpless, somewhat irritated.

Then, he asked Farida to leave the room, because he had to make a phone call. She was humiliated, but she would not get upset. She gave him the pretext he needed not to lose his honour and have a clear conscience.

Hitler's armies were invincible. They were moving relentlessly over Europe and Africa. The soldiers were tightening the vice around Iraq, the essential petrol bases for the British.

Jawad spoke to her less and less. He ran his fingers through her hair, hugged her. He sauntered from kitchen to bedroom to living room. Anissa served tea and coffee. He took a bite of a date and nibbled pastries. Farida noticed Jawad's forced courtesy. He could blow up any time. She wanted to avoid a confrontation; she did not want to utter a word too many.

The German troops were attacking every front, but Taha al Hachimi had the situation under control. The British had no intention of leaving Iraq.

FOR TWO WEEKS, JAWAD was nowhere to be found. Farida encouraged Fahim to call the police. Jawad was in hiding. Then one morning, at the end of March, a vehicle parked in front of the house. A man dressed in a black suit knocked on the door. Anissa answered.

"Farida?"

"No, Mrs. Farida is not ready."

"Anissa?"

"That's me."

"Mr. Jawad will be arriving today with his men. He must not be bothered at any cost."

"And Mrs. Farida?"

"It is most important that no one see her."

"And me?"

"You? Make some coffee and tea. Fahim will service the guests. Do as you are told. This is what Mr. Jawad asks of you."

Farida was in her bedroom listening. Afraid, she jerked Salim awake.

"We must get out."

Salim was dumbfounded.

"Where will we go?"

Once they had slipped into their clothes, she asked: "What are we to do now?"

There was no time to waste. A military vehicle stopped in front of the house. They had enough time to run downstairs.

The men asked Fahim: "Is this Mr. Jawad's residence?"

They forced their way inside. A second vehicle parked outside. Farida and Salim were curled in a corner and from the window they looked at the soldiers running. There were footsteps on the floor above. Chairs were moved, voices thundered. There was no laughter. Farida thought she recognized Rachid Ali rushing into the house. Silence. She then heard Jawad calling for Fahim. Two soldiers stood outside the window. Salim pulled Farida to the bed, and slid under the bed sheets.

Salim felt desire overcome him, a feeling that distracted him from any thought of death. Farida anticipated Salim's actions. She was sure of surviving.

As for Salim, this would be his final jump, the last moment of life. They were in love as if it was the first time they met. Passionately. Without pausing. Life was departing, deserting them. She was inexhaustible. This was going to be their last moment. He was indestructible. Their days were counted. Stopping could not be anything but a pause. Their bodies demanded rights, movement was mute, panting silenced. They had only their skin to protest with. They climbed toward forgetfulness with ardour. This meant crossing over death, and yet never reaching the end.

The noise above intensified. Footsteps. Boots hammered against the floor. Vehicles sped away. In a matter of seconds, there was tranquillity. Was this the end of a nightmare?

The following day, news on the radio announced Taha al Hachimi's resignation, and Rachid Ali's political takeover. Newspapers sprinkled details of the events. The Regent, the young King, and the Royal family took refuge in Iran. The army supported Rachid Ali. *Liwa Al Istaklal* was direct. "We are witnessing a coup d'état."

The army had taken over. The nationalist military handed over the country's authority to Rachid Ali. The Al Zawraa malha was crammed that week. Soldiers had packed the hall. Farida was welcomed with enthusiastic applause like in the old days.

"We are witnessing historical events," Anton repeated.

Jawad gave no sign of life. Still the newspapers kept mentioning his name. He was at the head of the region's police. *Liwa Al Istaklal* proposed him as the next Minister of the Interior in order to bring half-hearted individuals to heel. He had to especially keep under control the people who could possibly betray them, who would prevent the march of History.

There was a call to calm.

Rachid Ali had to explain his political program. Inside: there would be national unity. Wars without end against traitors. Outside: neutrality. Iraq was an ally of the British no more, nor of the Germans. No one mentioned this. Jawad kept his mouth shut. The Prime Minister ordered the British to evacuate their military bases within Iraq. The Iraqi forces were getting ready to advance toward Habbaniya and Fellouja. They would drive out the colonizer so as to reclaim sovereignty over the entire territory.

Events proceeded so rapidly that even Salim with his ear to the radio, reading three or four newspapers a day, could not make heads or tails about what was happening, or hope to explain it to a horrified Farida.

There was no news from Jawad.

One afternoon, without thinking about it, Farida phoned Jawad's office.

"His Excellence is not at home," the voice at the other end said.

What is to become of us? She thought but did not ask the question. Her eyes expressed a fear deeper than Salim's. She could do nothing for him. He was aware of it. He had dragged her along with him in his fall. They were alone: Jews without being Jews, victims without being part of the community of victims.

When darkness came, and not having made her usual trip to the malha, Farida cuddled up to Salim and forgot the world. They held one another into the night, speechless, freeing themselves of a weight they could not understand.

There was a celebration at the malha. Heading for battle, the Iraqi forces made their way to Habbaniya. The radio boomed with shouts of victory. Endless rallying via telegrams. All the leaders of every tribe, one after the other. The heroic army has pushed the occupying forces out of the nation's territory.

Other telegrams from rallying Jews followed. They named individuals. Iraqi among Iraqi. They were being rallied like everybody else. They were publicly expressing their loyalty. They backed the government, backed Rachid Ali. They wanted to free their national territory.

"Idiots," Salim told himself. "Free to kill. Defenceless. This is what they are demanding."

He knew he would have been the first to send a telegram, rallying like any other sheikh. Even if it would mean sending a telegram to the next government, no matter who that might be.

Radio-Berlin was jubilant. Joy never arrives alone. Victory on every front. Farida ventured one morning into the souk. It was a day like any other. Jews and Muslims alike were in their shops, standing behind the stalls. There they were, with clients. As long as they did not stand out, not being seen, not being heard. They were like everybody else. These people were afraid. They were defenceless. But no one was attacking them. Farida was relieved at not being part of any group, at not having more importance than anyone else in the community.

She was only a singer who was applauded during her singing at marriages. People were proud of her for being a Jewish woman. Yet she did not feel as belonging to their community. She was a foreigner to Jews. There would no longer be any weddings. The Jews celebrated bar mitzvahs in synagogues, only discreetly. They did not need her anymore. She was a symbol of celebration, feasts, happiness. The future as carefree living. There would be no partying anymore, no more celebration. Her place was in the malha now. Surrounded by Rachid Ali's soldiers. That is where the party would be held, where there would be celebrating. On stage, she would become absent to herself. She was neither Jewish, nor Muslim. It was Farida the singer they applauded. They were asking for more. There was no Salim, no Jawad, no Rachid Ali anymore. The army was accumulating victories, giving the British one lesson after another.

It was the second week of April. The beds were brought to the roof. The evening breeze was getting warm. Soon she would feel as though she was losing her breath. Salim expected nothing anymore. Late one afternoon, dressed in Anissa's clothes, Salim walked out alone all the way to Aadhamiya, and then off to Bab el Mouadham. Men and women went about their business, pretending there was no war. In front of Maydane, men stepped into the reserved quarter, cut off from the rest of the other citizens. This was their routine. In the distance, by Shamash school, students were gesticulating as they made their way out, conversing in their normal way.

Were they more frightened than the Muslims? He sensed their impatience, their expectancy. They were aware that victory was not a given. Like their parents, they were frightened. Victory might even be improbable, and defeat a possibility. Since the Jewish people found themselves isolated, like Salim was, they could speak and reveal their fears. Salim wondered if his father had gone to the synagogue, as he would have done before; if his mother had felt shame for her son. Did Naji ever mention his name? Did Najiah, a prisoner under the Karkouklis, blame him for all the evil that befell her?

Salim made his way back. Too scared to hail a cab, he jumped on the bus. He was exhausted by the time he got to his basement. He slept for a few hours. When he awoke, he heard Anissa and Farida's footsteps on the floor above. Farida had not come down to invite him upstairs. He being there, useless, dangerous, weighed on her, made her fidgety. She preferred, Salim told himself, that he would go away for a week, a month. He would return with gifts and stories to tell. She would receive him like a by-gone lover come back to her. He too wished to go away. He did not want to read on Farida's face the fear of finding no other refuge except silence.

When Salim climbed upstairs, Farida was sipping her tea. She was getting ready to leave. She stared at him as if he were a stranger, a passer-by, an outsider. She was not indifferent, nor was she hostile to him. She was simply absent.

"Are you off to the malha?"

"Yes, Anton is expecting to receive orders to shut the place down."

Salim did not ask for an explanation. He had guessed right. War was knocking at the door. The phone rang. It was Anton.

"No use coming. The malha has been shut down."

FARIDA

The war had been officially declared against Great Britain. Military planes flew over Baghdad dropping leaflets. Rachid Ali had formed a new cabinet. Nazi sympathizers had printed their pro-German leaflets. The radio repeated instructions and orders as to what to do: curfews to respect, forces mobilized, actions that might help the enemy to be avoided. Jews were walking home.

In the evening cafés were empty, streets deserted. Teenagers enrolled in the Futuwa, a militia gang, and every day these young arrested Jews, accusing them of sending distress signals to the British planes overhead. Victims were often innocent passers-by or shop owners who hid themselves behind shop windows. When they found themselves at the police headquarters, they would drop a dinar in the hands of the inspector. There were times when a person would be kept behind bars for a day or two and would have to pay up to a dozen dinars to be able to get back home. All actions and movements were questioned.

Farida pulled the opaque curtains across the windows giving onto the street. Salim was listening to Radio-London. The Iraqi were not progressing. They had been stopped at the entrance of the British army base. The British were losing on all fronts, except for one. In the evening Farida climbed to the roof. Salim went down into the basement. He knew this was the end of an era. This was the end of a period in his life. Would other periods follow?

He had no idea what to think. Every morning he would wake up tired. When Farida showed signs of frustration, inquiring about what he was going to do, Salim replied: "I am still alive."

Each day was a miracle. When would it come to an end? When drama and catastrophe would be exhausted, a new day would rise. He would be standing there. If so, in what state? In which place? He did not want to answer.

Every morning, Anissa would go to the market square and would come back crestfallen. What would she become? The Jews were leading the platoon. Christians, Assyrians, Armenians, and Kurds would be next. Jawad was no longer there to protect them.

When it came time, Fahim knew which party he belonged to. In the meantime, he kept his distance from Farida. He was not at the service of this Jewish woman, the colleague of a Christian woman. His orders came to him from his leader, His Excellency Jawad, the chief of Liwa's police force.

Salim was not saying a word about the situation. He had only his fear to share. With Farida's eyes reflecting fear back to him, fear doubled in size.

The sun was beating hard. Salim choked in his cell. The future he imagined was bursting. There would be dead bodies everywhere. People who would survive the explosion would be reborn one day. Salim was convinced that he would be one of the survivors. A new life awaited him. In the debris, his destiny would be reconstituted. He would walk out unharmed. In this new existence there would be no place for Farida. She was becoming excess baggage. He stared at her. Lost. Looking like a woman from his own family: his mother or one of his aunts. An elderly woman like any other elderly woman.

One morning an officer in plain clothes knocked at the door. His Excellency was announcing his coming visit. The man said that they had to prepare the house for His Excellency's stay there. They had to purchase provisions. The man turned around and left.

Farida demanded that these orders be repeated a number of times. She did not understand. What provisions? What stay? That very evening answers would be transmitted on radio. Rachid Ali and his government had taken flight for Iran. Military officers and persons of consequence had established a committee for interior security. This was Thursday. The day after offices would be closed. Saturday and Sunday would be Shavuot: the Jewish celebration of the Torah.

The city had shut its gates. There was no government in power. Farida was waiting for Jawad's arrival, Jawad the Saviour, Jawad the Guardian. Salim would be hiding in his basement cell, while Farida would be with her master, completely safe. Never had the city streets been so empty. The Jews locked themselves in their homes. Muslims stood on roofs whispering. No one wanted to be accused of sending information to the enemy.

The new committee communicated their press releases on radio pleading for people to stay calm. Life gradually settled back into routine. Rachid Ali was no longer the Prime Minister. The Germans had not come to save him. Hitler had other worries now. War against the Russians was next. They had encircled Iraq's capital. Troops were crossing over the city gates, their movements heard by every citizen. Gunshots thundered. Teenagers of the Futuwa charged against men and women who were walking out of the synagogue, dressed in their finest clothes in honour of the Shavuot. Soldiers were screaming: "These Jews are celebrating Iraq's defeat."

The British army stood outside the city waiting. The Iraqi troops were lost in a fog.

"Who are our leaders? Who will give us orders?"

The city was without a leader; it became a haven for killers and bandits. Bedouin hordes rushed out of their tents and pilfered shops that Jewish owners had abandoned.

The radio proclaimed that the interior security committee was responsible for giving orders. But gun fire would not die down.

One Sunday morning, in his police uniform, revolver in his holster, Fahim took up his position at the front of the door, acting of his own accord as a defender. There was no one above to tell him what to do.

In her room, Farida lifted the corner of a curtain and peeped outside. Men, women, and children were walking in groups, hauling furniture and goods not belonging to them. This was nothing less than a sacking. Children's backs were bent under the weight of a chair or table put there by their parents. Some children would drop the loot which an adult would then pick up. This was an endless procession of men and women yelling injunctions at their children lugging heavy booty in spite of their fatigue.

The Sulaykh ghetto consisted of no more than 20 buildings; each had been plundered. If the ransacking would not stop, the same fate awaited Christians, scattered here and there, followed by Muslims. Looters noticed Fahim standing on the horizon. He could do nothing to stop the thieves. If a young boy sneered or mocked Fahim, he would lower his hand onto his revolver. Nervous adults reprimanded their children.

During an evening transmission, the Governor of Liwa announced the Regent's edict: "The police will shoot on sight any pillager."

A curfew was imposed once more.

The phone rang that evening. It was Jawad. He whispered that he would be coming over. Salim was not afraid. Jawad was about to join the legion of fugitives. Farida was aware that Muslims could kill one another on one day and on the next become friends at the expense of the Jews. She stood in the dark for a moment. Once the storm dissipated, Jawad would express his gratitude. The phone rang again. It was Jawad, his voice firm, almost gleeful. On the way to Iran, he would be able to forget. The storm will pass.

The chief of police was the cornerstone of the regime, openly connected to Rachid Ali. His time would return.

Relieved, Farida could not contain her sadness and anxiety. Jawad tried to calm her, reassuring her by repeating the latest news.

The army and police resurfaced. The Bedouins scampered back to their tents. Muslims would go back on the street as rulers. The radio predicted peace and the empowerment of the regime. The Regent would select Jamil Al Madfaï as the Prime Minister. They would institute an inquiry commission. A few days passed before men and women ventured back on the streets, mistrusting the police and soldiers, not sure if they could sigh with relief or not. Afterwards would come the counting of the dead, the wounded, the victims of thievery.

For a week, there would be nothing. Anissa went to the market. Fahim in his uniform admired the sunset. Farida would not speak much, spending hours dusting and rearranging furniture. Salim refused to shave.

"There is no wake," he told her, forcing a smile.

"Not yet. I've got no idea. Now that I have a new face."

The following morning he slipped into a suit, put on a sidara, and stepped into the daylight.

Farida had no time to call him back. He vanished into the horizon. Whatever reasons he had to worry disappeared. He was swept by a conflagration. What could happen to them at this moment? Salim returned later that afternoon. He had the same joy written on his face as when he first walked into the office. She cried her anger for no real reason.

"I was worried sick."

But she was not worried at all. He wondered if it was indifference or the conviction that the threat was a story of the past. He spoke of his stroll, and how he took the bus downtown. The souk was busy with activity. Life had returned. The Battawiyeen quarter had been spared. The hordes of invaders had no time to usurp it. Their families had been unscathed.

At sunrise, a car parked below the window. Salim did not budge. Farida glanced in assent.

The world had been turned upside down. The worst was now behind them. Anton knocked, excusing himself.

"I didn't want to phone."

"Come in," Farida said. "It's the first time that you honour this house with your presence. Salim, my cousin."

He was to re-open the malha in a few weeks. He wanted to publicize a new program. She would become a star. Life was starting over. Anissa served tea. Salim nodded, saying "yes" and "no". He was a cousin and willingly participated to this conversation.

"I have something to tell you," Anton said, glancing at Salim.

"I have to go," Salim said.

"Don't come back too late," she said.

As soon as they found themselves alone, Anton said: "It is Jawad who sends me."

"Jawad? Why didn't he come himself? Where is he?"

"Jawad came to see me before leaving. He asked me to take care of you, in case something unexpected happened. I had to keep silent. I didn't have to hide myself. Officers will be clients at the malha."

"Talk to me about Jawad," she said.

"Yes. He decided to leave with Rachid Ali and his ministers.

Though he had obeyed the government's directions, he believed he was being tracked down. Once in Khanaquin, he changed his mind. Defeated, men are not a pretty sight. Rachid Ali's companions were no exception. Intelligent as he was, Jawad understood that this was not his world. The chief of police in Khanaquin was a former assistant of his. He took him in, but Jawad was broke. His family in Baghdad was unable to deal with what was going on. I would have lent him money, but the malha had shut down and I was … I don't need to explain, Farida."

"He sent you here to ask me for money? Right?"

"Not really. If you want to lend me three or four hundred dinars … a loan."

"I don't hide that sort of cash under my pillow. But let me see what I can do."

"I told Jawad that this house was his. He can live here, rent it, sell it."

"You suggested to him to ask me for rent?"

"Farida, you're insulting me. Who do you take me for? Did I worm myself into your life?"

EVERY MORNING SALIM WOULD take a walk. From day to day, he grew bolder. People did not recognize him, and so he was able to visit shops and stop in at cafés. One Saturday morning, he even helped with the Shabbat at the recently erected Meir Toeg synagogue. The rabbi accused the community of not respecting the laws to the letter. Women did not go to the Mikveh on a monthly basis to get purified. Men did not respect the Shabbat by going to work and smoking. Salim thought he was right, as he had thought his mother right for scolding him whenever he did something wrong. He felt relieved. When he would be free, he would obey the wisdom the Torah teaches. He was happy to be invisible, being able to vanish from scene to scene, no longer a prisoner of the living. There were mornings when he would venture out on the street of the Karkouklis. He would be reborn. He would one day tell them all that he was here, and that he would seek revenge. Against whom? Against what? He smiled and became the child scolded by his mother.

He sat in a café listening to two Jewish men discussing travelling. Rachid Street was not far from the malha. He came back the following day and noticed that one of the men was sitting alone. Salim went to sit at the neighbouring table.

"I'm from Kut," he said. "Life for Jews has become unbearable."

The man replied with a friendly smile: "It's no better in Baghdad. But many of us keep our pipedreams alive."

"The idiots," Salim said. "There are no Jews in Kut anymore. We were spared in Farhoud. Not because of any goodness. News simply did not reach there on time. The next time they will erase any trace of their existence. I've come here, but Baghdad is no answer."

"Oh no. It's even worse here."

"I ...," Salim said, paused. "I only want to leave. But I know no one."

"Don't you have a family?"

"I have a cousin. A cobbler. Shlomo Cohen. I went to his house in Qambar Ali. Dead. Assassinated. He and his entire family. A wife and their two girls. One of the two had been promised to me. Some Muslims did not see it that way. Neighbours told me that the four had their throats slit. They didn't tell me what they did to the girls. I can only imagine. Do you call this living?"

"No, it isn't."

"What about a Jew in this country? Since my arrival, all I've been thinking of is going away. I know no one who can help. The other day at a watermelon stand, I heard a man say that we could go to Iran. Without papers, without a passport. From there they take you in charge and take you to your home."

Salim hesitated before smiling at the man.

"I spoke to the man, but he was not interested. As though I were an informer, or working for the police. I wasn't upset with him. One can never be careful enough."

Salim waited, but the man did not move. Salim decided not to push any further and switched to his discovery of

Baghdad, his walks along the river, and his desire to leave it all. The man listened silently. He nodded and smiled.

As soon as he came back home, he noticed that Farida was frazzled. The malha was about to open once again. Anton had chosen her as its promotional voice. Farida: a new program for the great national singer. A poster would be circulated in every café on Bank Street. She was expecting a modest attendance. Jews rarely went to the malha. With the Faroud gone, they would not easily celebrate in public. The army no longer boasted proud and arrogant officers. Who would win the country back? The hall was filled with military men in plain clothes, Christians, and a few Jews. There were also young men in abundance. When Farida walked on stage, the audience broke out in loud applause. An ovation. Was it she or the end of the war they were cheering? She began to sing with a lucidity she detested in herself. She was the spectator of her own show.

When she came back on stage for the second set, the murmur of voices escalated, requesting the well-known songs of the past. She introduced the first song in her deep voice. She sang with clarity and control, overwhelmed with emotions surging from past times. She was no longer there, fading behind an unquenchable desire that she could neither command nor hold back. Her singing turned into a call. Without regret, without nostalgia. She touched the primordial sadness of living and the difficulty of life. The hall fell into total silence. A whisper grew into a deep voice, swelling louder into a supplication for the return, for the struggle against absence.

When she walked off stage, she was totally exhausted and collapsed in a chair.

"Farida," someone called to her.

Anton was on his knees. The audience was screaming for an encore.

"Farida."

She heard her name. Space vanished. Distance shrunk. "My name is Farida." She was Farida. She needed no one to remind her of this name, no one need to repeat it. Tomorrow, she would be back on stage and her voice of freedom would lift her, quivering with life force.

Salim became a regular at the café. When he caught sight of the two men, he rushed in and sat at the opposite end of the room and waited. It turned out to be an entire week's wait. The two men finally nodded to him and went back to their conversation. One evening he got there earlier than usual.

One of the men was sitting alone.

Salim got up and walked up to him.

"I need to talk to you. I want to get out of here. Can you help me?"

The man appeared deeply preoccupied.

"Why?" he said speaking like a sigh.

"I wish to cross the border. I have no passport."

"Where will you go?"

"Where? Are you laughing at me? I don't want to go to Syria or Turkey … nor to Saudi Arabia."

"Do you want to find a home in Iran?"

"At the beginning. But no more than a few months."

"You're waiting?"

"My target is Jerusalem. Or Tel Aviv."

A smile spread over the man's face.

"I'm Saddiq."

"I will have the money you ask for."

"I'll see what I can do. We'll speak next week. Where do you live?"

"I live with my sister-in-law's sister. In Sulaykh. Here's my phone number."

"We'll talk later."

The next day the phone rang. Farida answered.

"Salim, it's for you."

She was not frightened.

"Yes," Salim answered. There was breathing, then the line went dead.

He understood and wished to share his secret with Farida. Jewish men were about to help him. He noticed compassion in her eyes, in a woman he was leaving behind, the pity of a woman forsaken.

"You don't want to talk to me."

"Of course, I do. This is all I want."

He had become distant, a brother, a colleague from the past, an intimate friend inscribed in her memory, outside of time. With the hope of bringing her to his side, he took her in his arms, but she was absent. He caressed her mechanically though he hoped to bring joy to her body. In the memory of gestures, he recognized her one touch at a time. He saw himself moving. Was this the woman he loved? The woman he had loved? Was she just a shadow? He wrapped his arms around her, and he felt sorry for not recognizing himself in her, as someone from his past.

Would he reveal to her his plans to leave? That things were about to change? What did he have to say that could encourage her to accompany him? Or maybe that he might join her later? But he was not even able to tell her he loved her.

Jawad sent his messages via messengers. If a shy Anton stood longer than was necessary beside Farida, she would break the charm by asking ironically: "So when did you last see Jawad?"

"Well ...," Anton stuttered, hesitant and nervous about passing her a message. "Jawad needs money."

"I sent him five hundred dinars."

"It's not enough. The worse is that he will not borrow any more money."

A woman, a Jewish woman, a lover, a singer. What humiliation.

"He wants to sell the house."

"A great idea," she exclaimed. "I'll buy it. At the going rate."

"This is what he wants. You'll be able to deduct his debts."

"Here's an advance, a thousand dinars, before the negotiations of the selling price. Take them from my pay."

The malha had come back to life. Thanks to Farida. That she was a Jewish woman played in her favour. She would keep Fahim and Anissa, who had been an ally. Her servant. Jawad was far away and would no longer control her life. His shadow once so imposing faded away. He had lived his life without paying much attention to the traces he would leave behind. From the start she thought the house was hers. After all these years, Jawad had been unable, perhaps, never wanted to be master. Dealing with his inferiors perhaps. With her ... If he would resurface one day, she would not be there to welcome him.

The sadness, the solitude, without a friend to share her happiness, she felt relief at finding herself at last free of his weight. Farida would sing in the evening. People would come to listen to her sing, bringing along a presence that translated into total freedom. She begged Anton to ask a dellal, an intermediary, to evaluate Jawad's house.

"That's done already. I've got the price on paper."

Ten thousand dinars. It's crazy. No one will want to purchase it at that price. In a year or two if ... but she had neither the energy nor the wish to start bargaining. Money came to her easily. She asked for one hundred, one hundred and fifty dinars for her evening shows. Be it for a wedding or at the malha, she was no longer counting. Anton would hand over her pay.

"Ask Jawad if the price is right for him."

"I tell you it is."

The news did not surprise Farida. Jawad was broke. She knew once his energy was found anew, he could return to meet her without ever mentioning the house, the money, or the past. He would be frank, and have no shame.

"All you need to do is get the cheques and documents ready. Are they ready?"

Anton laughed; so did she.

"You knew," she said.

"I know you, Farida. And I know Jawad."

She had decided to tell Salim the news, but on that evening she chose not to mention a thing. Why humiliate him? In another life, in another world, she would have loved Jawad, perhaps even have found the right words to tell him so. She loved the house. She walked around it. She would be the owner. Nothing would change. She could see herself exclaiming to Salim: "This is my house now."

She found herself feeling ridiculous. Better to say nothing. Salim walked the city freely. He stopped in front of the Karkoukli house, wanting to be caught. He was fascinated by the abyss, frightening as it was. As soon as the door to the house opened, he ran away.

In Battawiyeen he would often stroll by his house. Silence. His mother had died. Farida had listened to him talk about it once. His father could no longer walk. He prayed without moving. Naji? Maybe he was married by now. He looked for his shadow, a vision of his face before he went away.

His routine consisted of sitting at the café, listening to the radio. It was Farida singing. He could recognize her voice anywhere. But this voice was not the same voice he had heard when he woke up in the morning or going to bed at the night. This was the woman he was looking for; this was the woman he loved as a melody.

Saddiq waved at him, but walked on by. Then, one evening, he came up to him with his friend.

"Let's get out of here. We have to talk to you."

The warm evening breeze announced the end of summer. They were strolling by the river on Abou Nouas Street, with no one around.

"Salim," Sami said, "we know your history. Where you come from, and where you are now."

Salim was upset, could not utter a word.

"We're not informers for the police," Saddiq said.

"That is of no interest for us," Sami added.

"Can you have five hundred dinars in two weeks?"

"The money is necessary," Saddiq said.

"You'll be leaving soon, in a month or so. You have to give us the money beforehand. You'll need more money for expenses along the way."

"But ..."

"I know," Sami said. "We can't give you a receipt for this money. You must trust us."

"Of course, yes. Is it a certainty?"

"Totally. You have to keep in mind your circumstances. Do you have a family in Teheran?"

"Teheran? A cousin, I think. But he doesn't know me."

"No trouble. Just in case. All is set up from the start."

"What about Teheran?"

"That's another story. We'll speak about it when it's time to do so."

"You give us the money," Saddiq said, "and we promise you that we'll place you in the hands of the Shah."

The two men laughed. Salim laughed as well, even if laughter seemed uncalled for and somewhat ridiculous.

"One has to eat and sleep in the meantime. You'll need all your energy."

Salim knew nothing of these men. Who did they represent? But he had no choice. He had to go. This was the time to do so. How was he going to tell Farida? If they arrested him, they would retrace the money to her. Was this really the end for them? Was it time to analyze the results? At night, he caressed Farida, as though she were a fragile and precious jewel. He saw her in the future where memory would people a boundless absence.

"How beautiful you are."

She was laughing, and she was happy.

"What is wrong with you? You've gone mad."

"You're beautiful, Farida."

"I know."

"No, you don't know. It is I who is telling you so."

He was becoming moody. She did not want to have to understand, did not want to help him. They were fighting against the ephemeral, by building the memory of this present instant, so deeply engraved in absence.

"I'll never forget you."

"I hope so. No way. In any case, I've no intention of leaving you."

"But I ... if ...," he said turning his head aside.

"What? You?"

Her voice grew sombre, fading into the landscape. She knew it. She always knew. It was quite possible that Saddiq and Sami had come in contact with him.

"I'm leaving, Farida. I'm going away."

He gently dropped his lips on Farida's wet cheeks. She was weeping; there were tears behind her laughter. How could he forget how unique and fine she was? She wanted to transform this break-up into a joyful event without sadness. They would be free. They would once again find themselves and they would be in love. They would reinvent their love. They would be searching for neologisms to express this love. They were wordless, hugging one another. He was scared that by moving he would disrupt the order of the world. He had at last come to balance himself in a precarious harmony. He realized that he was for the first time experiencing an emotion, similar to the emotion he had experienced when they had come to arrest him.

"Will you come?" he asked.

"Yes. I will come to see you wherever you might be."

"There is no future for Jews in this country. Sooner or later, we will be ordered to leave."

"To go where?"

"We'll have our own country."

"You too?" she muttered dreamily.

"What me too? Who are you thinking of?"

"No one. You know that. There's no one. There will never be another."

She did not enjoy the emphatic tone of her voice. It gave her the impression of singing off-key or of having lost her voice.

"You will come?"

She was overtaken by an urge to scream: "Stop being so down!" But she contented herself to whisper: "Yes, yes. I will come."

"I love you, Farida."

His voice cracked. He hated this sentimental state that brought him back to himself, to his own limits, that reduced the amplitude of what he thought he was feeling: his love was immense and enigmatic.

"You have to eat something. You have to rest."

"I've got all the time in the world. I can say that I have all my life for that."

They smiled.

"We will find you," she said.

She fell back into her role: the woman, the wife, the older sister. She was getting him ready for the trip. He would be leaving after all. Alone on this uncertain journey. She wanted to sink her face into the pillow and let her tears flow. But she shouldn't allow her despair to be revealed. She protected him, pulled him from his world, from adversity. And he was her armour, her protection. It was she who would lay her head on his shoulder. There in her big house, then before hundreds of admirers, she would stand straight up, alone. Beware that she might flinch. Everyone would want to kill her. She fought against panic, unable to exorcize it.

She hummed a song:

I will never be without you,
You will always be there.
Where are you?
There you are, waving
At the end of the road.

This was her way of not belittling their feelings. Beyond and above their caresses, she had to translate awkward gestures with words.

"Salim," she said.

"Yes."

"You gave me the most beautiful years of my life."

She was unsettling the balance.

"But this is not the end, Farida. I'm not dead. I'm not ... You'll see. I'll build a house for you. We'll live together. We'll have children."

"Tomorrow I'll pick up the money."

It was not necessary to ask her if she was aware of what was happening.

Saddiq had been following her for some time now. He had come to visit her, first at the malha, and then elsewhere.

The next day, he caught her sewing the sleeves of a jacket where she had hidden a few dinars.

"At the bank they'll take you for a pilgrim coming back from Kerbela."

He had no desire to laugh. She prepared a meal. Rice of every kind.

"You must put on weight."

For Farida, it became a slightly spicy game. First, forgetting his departure; then, her coming solitude.

"You prefer to see me as free as a prisoner running in handcuffs."

"Of course," she said.

She wondered if this was all true. She was not sure. Nothing could replace his voice, smell, laughter, caresses, the endless nights of lovemaking. She refused to imagine that she might never experience such moments again. That would be betraying him before he even walked out of the door. She would not exchange her life for another.

"You can't be replaced," she said and felt like crying. Any expression of fidelity would indicate that she was frightened of his leaving. He did not stop repeating: "You'll join me later."

He was aware that his life was in crisis, that he had to reinvent his existence, that he would have to transform himself and be reborn a new man, a novel character. If not, he would not survive. No one expected to find him in a country where he knew no one, and did not speak the language. "You'll come." She would be his armour and his supporter. What would he do with her? A woman he was not married to. He told himself that he would get back in the race. He would build a house for Farida, and hire servants. Teheran was a step away. In a few months he would be gone to a place where the world would be different. There, he would be a new man. His past would be engulfed by the past of an entire population. They would have forgotten the derisory act for which he found himself in prison. From there on, he would write Naji to tell him what was happening, to Najiah to tell her that ... but all of that was so far away.

He was here.

Farida was unable to be truly present. Her attention was directed to the following day, to the return trip. What return trip? He would never be coming back. This was the end. She felt her throat tighten. She could not breathe. He had everything to lose in the gaining of a new life. He could die along the way, for instance, being killed by the guide, or by being held up by the customs officers. Poor Salim. She was confident. He was tough. They could not lock Salim in a cage. He might seem submissive. But he was preparing his next move. Discreetly. She would be joining him. Where? In an unknown country. They would become a couple. She would stop singing. They would have children. At this point in her life, a dream could turn into a nightmare.

Just thinking about quitting her career as a singer threw her into pangs of anxiety. Never had such a thought crossed her mind.

"I'm losing my voice. The day will come when I'll not be able to sing."

That was the unthinkable. The applause gave her confidence. Never had she been so conscious of her power, not only in front of her public, but also in herself.

She controlled her voice, playing with the melody; she was enjoying herself.

"I'll be coming to you," she insisted in order to push aside the sadness and anxiety that were creeping over her.

In this unknown country, she would sing melodies. She would learn the new lyrics that she had to get a grip on, moulding them to her voice. People would applaud, and the public would offer her an ovation.

At the café, Saddiq nodded to Salim and walked on by, as if he did not know him. The day before, Salim had handed him the money in bills of five and ten dinars. The following day, walking before him into the café, Saddiq hesitated. "The numbers add up," he said. "Prepare yourself."

"I'm ready. When?"

"We'll let you know."

He found Farida standing in the shadows, tears in her eyes.

"Excuse me. I've got no idea what is happening to me. You'll be gone. I'll have no one anymore."

"I used to be in charge, Farida."

"Don't say that. You've got no idea what is at stake here."

"You'll be coming to see me."

Her voice cracked.

"Listen, Salim. You're leaving. You'll be gone."

"We'll meet again."

There was lack of belief in her voice. He wanted it all to end soon. He was impatient to get to the other side. Which side? Yonder? There, he would be phoning her, and she would answer. To go away, and then to return.

Farida said smiling, resolute as she used to be: "I've decided to purchase a car. I visited a number of concessionaries' display showrooms: Chevrolet at Lawee; Oldsmobile at Menachi Machaal; Pontiac at Shafic Ades. I know nothing about cars. But Anton advises I get an Oldsmobile."

She stared at him. Dismayed, not knowing, once the surprise was gone, if he would be happy or disappointed, relieved or helpless. He had not gone yet …

"I'll need to hire a driver. Fahim counselled I hire his brother-in-law."

"He who …" Salim tried to swallowed his saliva.

"Yes. He doesn't work for the police anymore. Jawad not being there, he's been going through some tough times."

When Anton transferred the ownership documents to Farida, he added with a strange smile: "You're the owner now. The house is yours. Jawad is glad that this house belongs to you. He would have preferred to give it to you at no cost."

"But he has given it to me as a gift."

She had a hard time imagining herself as an owner. The house was hers, yet she was not the owner of her own body, or her own voice. Her voice could betray her at any moment. It could break on her. Her bank account was something unreal to her. With Farhoud's departure, Anton lost faith in himself, half-obsequiously, half-beseechingly, repeated: "Without you, there can be no malha."

He was at her service. He owed her his daily gain and social status.

She could have exploited this new situation, and turned Anton into her servant. Slavery disgusted her. In the worst case, she would have been lost. He was the person who kept her on her two feet. From now on, no one would be controlling her. She had her house. She had the malha. She had her servants. She would soon have her automobile and her personal driver. She would not need to report to anyone. Not to a father, not to a husband. Not even to a lover. Her fame preceded her. She saw herself on stage, facing an audience excited before she opened her mouth. She refused contracts for engagements at weddings. Organizers tried to get Anton to change her mind. But she said "no" and she never went back on her decision. It was not a question of money. She did not need much. Was she hoping to be a Jewish woman with a husband and a home? Compared to young greenhorns Salim was a giant. She had never wanted anything from life. She had no regrets. She had no reason to have regrets.

Silence followed as soon as he walked into her life. She was a myth, a legend, but found no joy in inciting admiration and respect from a distance. How could she believe in fame if she doubted her own voice? Was it truly her voice?

SAMI LOOKED FOR SALIM at the café. When he caught sight of him, he made his way to him.

"Follow me. Wait for me to go out."

Sami waited for him at the corner of the block.

"Tomorrow's the day. Four in the morning. On Rachid Street. By the new bridge. A suitcase, and nothing else. There will be four of you in the car. Five with the driver.

"Where are we going?"

Sami broke into a nervous laughter.

"I thought you had a meeting with Reza Shah."

"I do," Salim replied quivering. "By which road do we get there?"

"There is only one road. Tomorrow you'll be in Khanaquin. And from there, a guide will help you. Better not speak."

"What about the others?"

"You'll meet them. They are like you."

"They are ..."

"Neither Kurds, nor Talkeefs. Just like you."

"And once we get there?"

"You'll be brought to meet the Shah."

"Sami," Salim whispered, anxious and angry.

"Don't worry." Sami tried to calm him. He was more nervous than Salim.

"I'm not worried. What happens once we get there?"

"Don't worry about tomorrow. You'll be given instructions at the bridge. One thing at a time."

Salim grew thoughtful.

Luckily, Farida would be on stage at the malha, while he was on the road to Sulaykh. He would leave without attracting attention. He would hardly have time to kiss Farida farewell.

When he came back to the house, he noticed a nightgown.

"I was waiting for you," Farida said, forcing a smile.

She knew, having been warned. It was important that this moment, being their last, would be inscribed in her memory with its splendour, sensitivity, and beautiful gestures. He imagined himself abroad, thinking back at this moment, feeling as though he was one person too many. She was beautiful, fullness of breasts and hips. He desired her but not now; rather, in a time to come. This was the life he was leaving behind, a life from which he would detach himself bit by bit. Farida had become a dimension of everyday life. The thought that she would not be there in the morning, in the evening, was like a wound.

"You're leaving tomorrow," she whispered. "I'll be waiting for you."

She was searching for that joy in her tone but she was unable to conceal the emotion she felt facing death, absence, something without end, without limits. The earth was moving under her feet. She had to rediscover the meaning of words, reality.

"I have often thought about this moment," he said.

They exchanged looks. Immediately experienced total complicity. Consciousness rose after lengthy, loving embraces. Words on their respective lips completed one another, until words became unnecessary. It had always been this way. Only this time was perhaps their last time. Would he ever again express his love for her? Waiting for her to give him guarantees? Declaration become futile. No one had loved as much as he. No woman had ever given herself to love as much as she. What terms would be needed to explore this victory? How to recognize victory?

"I was waiting for this moment," he said, "to tell you, Farida, that we will meet again in another country which we will create with our hands. We will build our home. We will begin a new life. No one will ever point their finger at us. No one will envy us. No one will hate us. We will speak our own language. The language we will learn. Each word will become meaningful, the meaning we will give to it. Every evening I will be there when you come back from work. We will have children, boys and girls, proud of their father and mother. You will start singing again. In the old and new language. You'll find modern words of love that no one has ever pronounced before. You will sing them to your husband and children, to your people, discovered and found anew. I will be happy working with my hands. Our house will not be for us. We will build it for our children who will grow with dignity and who will be proud to belong to a community and to be free men."

Farida listened with eyes bright, staring into the unknown that she believed she understood. She felt like smiling as she had done on their very first day. Poor Salim. He was lulling himself with discourse.

"Don't worry, my love. You stir the dead with words. Can you see how fragile these are?"

She admired not so much eloquence, but his determination. She ignored sarcasm, rocked by lyrics of a song she recognized, a lost melody that rendered words useless. He struggled with death, expressing his love for her. Salim believed in the future, in the country to be created, in the family to come. He risked his life, but he had no choice. Living in the shadows, he did not believe he deserved love. His self-respect seemed futile.

There were certain nights when he, the prisoner, came to believe Farida was happy in her accessible body, illuminated by vitality, transforming him into an object, into a small, obedient pet.

Faced with scorn, she had to step back. Otherwise her self-love would turn into self-loathing.

"Farida, I'll give you everything. My love, my sweet one. With you I have courage to invent a country all of our own. I have the need to love you, to tell you I love you."

She told herself that he was speaking for speaking sake. This began to annoy her.

"I love you still. I have never stopped loving you."

"I know. But could you? I am nothing. Not even a shade."

"Salim, I know who you are."

"Oh Farida, my days are counted. If ever I get out of this experience alive, I will tell you that I love you."

He was about to add: "My gratitude, my gratitude" – but didn't.

Such words would have antagonized her. He chose to say nothing more.

"Salim, it is not over."

It was her turn to play the role of comforter, blossoming with words. But she stopped.

"I've not brought any LP by you in my suitcase. If ever they arrest me, I don't want them to punish you."

"I risk nothing. I want you beside me. I want you to be my man."

He took her in his arms, spending hours in an embrace. They experienced pain, anxiety, not to reduce it to discomfort.

He could not imagine their reunion. He saw her in all her splendour, cast in the future, when beauty would glow with a love very much alive.

Salim had hired a taxi the night before. Fahim carried the suitcase to the parked taxi. Farida held Salim by the shoulders, and said: "My brother, my brother, may God protect you."

Anissa and Fahim were standing in the doorway. Salim climbed into the taxi. Farida walked up to the car and shut the door. The car drove away. Farida, exhausted, sat down on the stairway, and wept until there were no more tears to shed. Anissa and Fahim went inside. Farida would continue to think of Salim. Her spirit went haywire, looked at the ground. Carrying some weight, disciplined ants marching in single file. She slowly regained consciousness of her skin, of her arms and legs. She would glance at the road and the cars taking men and women lost in their thoughts. She forgot her own presence, placed her hands on her arms, as though she were hurting. This is how days would come and go. She would sleep and she would wake up. Salim would send her a letter, after having arrived safely. What a man. Waiting. He had touched the bottom of the abyss and, unbroken, had climbed out. She stood; she was not unhappy. She felt emptiness, integral. She found refuge there, afraid, trying to run away, absence weighing her down. It was not Salim, but the entire world that hated her. But she must not succumb to this fascination of emptiness.

She conjured the past, willingly detailed each moment of her life, one by one, pulling them all to the surface, as proof of her breathing, of her power to walk and speak. She recalled her aunt, her first meeting with Salim. She did not have the right to desire, let alone dream.

What a journey! She was the owner of a house, of furniture.

People were screaming her name. They were applauding. Her name was a symbol of power, which she was unable to exploit fully. She owed nothing to anyone. She walked into her house, and went to stand behind a window, looking at the river. It was getting colder. Soon it would be winter.

The malha found her a stage for winter. She was shivering, happy that her body had become a symbol. She was alive. Jawad? He was gone forever. Her aunt? Her uncle? Gone. Her parents? Unknown. She had the malha. She would have a car and her own personal driver. She owed nothing to anyone. Salim? He would be coming back – to a specific place, at a specific time. Elsewhere. Alone. She needed no one. She did not even have the need to dream. She was free, she was alone. The balance sheet was satisfactory. The sun would rise. She would welcome the sunrays, an original warmth, a breath for a birthing. The air would thin; she would hyperventilate. Her throat would be tightened by a foreign, imprecise sensation.

What if life were an illusion?

ABOUT THE AUTHOR

Born in Iraq, Naïm Kattan moved to Montreal in 1954 where he quickly established himself as a strong participant in the province's intellectual life, especially in the area of literary studies. Novelist, short story writer and critic, Kattan has published more than 30 books, a few of which have been translated into English, including *Farewell, Babylon: Coming of Age in Jewish Baghdad*, *The Neighbour and Other Stories*, *Reality and Theatre*, and *A.M. Klein: Poet and Prophet*. While not born in Quebec, Kattan's cultural heritage, that of the Jewish minority in an Arab country, has made him particularly sensitive to the problems and aspirations of the French-speaking minority in English-speaking North America. Today, Kattan shares his time between Montreal and Paris.

ABOUT THE TRANSLATORS

Educator, religious studies scholar, and art critic, Montrealer Norman Cornett, Ph.D., teaches at universities throughout North America and Europe. He forms the subject of a documentary by Alanis Obomsawin. His translations appear in leading literary journals including *Canadian Literature, Rampike, Literary Review of Canada, ARC*, and *Windsor Review*. For more information, please go to http://haveyouexperienced.wordpress.com/.

Writer, editor, translator, publisher, filmmaker, Antonio D'Alfonso is the author of over 30 books. His novel *Un vendredi du mois d'août* won the Trillium Award in 2005. His feature film *Bruco* won best director award and best foreign film award at the New York International Independent Film Festival in 2010. His film *Antigone* (an adaptation of Sophocles' play) won the Bronze award at the Prestige Film Festival. Aside from his own award-winning writing, he has translated some of Quebec's finest authors.

Printed in April 2015
by Gauvin Press,
Gatineau, Québec